FIXIN' TO GET KILLED

The sun was well up when Belsher's riders wheeled their mounts away from the desert trail and headed toward the hidden entrance that led into the valley. The men, obviously gunmen and not cowhands, were surprised when Rocklin and MacCrue stepped out in front of them. They pulled up and one of them said, "What the hell?"

"It's all over for Belsher," MacCrue said. "Is it worth stretching rope for murder? Be smart, ride into town and tell them what you know."

"You must be loco," said one of the men. Then he turned in his saddle and said, "Hell, boys, it's only six to two," and went for his gun.

Rocklin and MacCrue pulled iron, but not before the gunslicks were attacking hell-for-leather, every gun ablaze . . .

150

SILENT RIDER

Jack Aintry

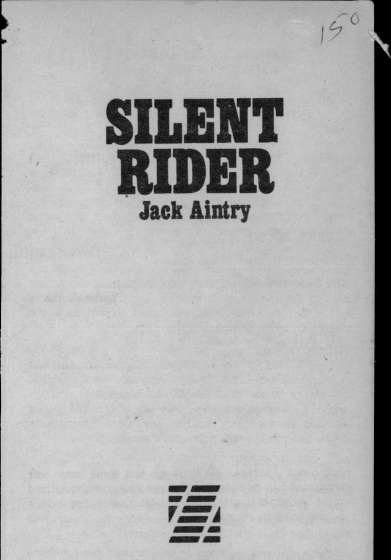

ZEBRA BOOKS
KENSINGTON PUBLISHING CORP.

ZEBRA BOOKS

are published by

Kensington Publishing Corp.
475 Park Avenue South
New York, NY 10016

First printing: June, 1988

Printed in the United States of America

Chapter 1

Rocklin pulled up at the top of an abrupt rise and got his first look at Sweetwater Valley.

It was beautiful, what he could see of it, with vast areas of tan and green stretching along the bottom land, and forest stretching up the slopes toward the surrounding mountains. It looked small in the hazy afternoon, but Rocklin knew it was at least thirty miles long and ten miles wide.

He took field glasses from his saddlebags and studied the scene before him for a long time. Then he took a map from a leather folder and studied that, deciding that the ranch house and outbuildings tucked into the side of a cliff about ten miles away to the east was the MacCrue place, the Bar M. The grass, high and thick, was turning a soft brown at the higher elevations but was still green along Sweetwater Creek. There was a fair number of cattle scattered over the land. A peaceful look-ing valley.

But Rocklin knew that at least a dozen men had died suddenly and violently there in just the past six months. He had studied that situa-tion too, and he was riding into it.

His horse, a sturdy buckskin that he natu-rally called "Buck"—although not within the hearing of anyone else—was studying the new terrain too, in his own way. He was looking around, tossing his head a bit, his ears swivel-ing front and back and his nostrils quivering. He had been with Rocklin quite a spell, and when his rider came alert, he came alert. It worked the other way around too.

With only the slightest of movements, Rock-lin nudged the horse around to look back out over the desert. It was startling. In all his time in the West, Rocklin hadn't seen such sudden change. He had been aware ever since he left the stage stop in the early morning that he had been very gradually climbing. The desert had changed some, cooled off just a touch and turned a bit green. Far back, there had been relentlessly hot days, warm nights and nothing but sand and rocks and alkali, endless sage-brush, creosote bushes and a few hedgehog cactus and jumping cholla. Now there were scattered juniper, yucca and even an occasional touch of color in the reddish-orange flower of the ocotillo.

The slightest touch of breeze brushed the back of Rocklin's neck and he relaxed in the saddle, letting his gaze wander across the incredible desert. The idea would never have occurred to him — he wasn't a deep-thinking kind of man — but Rocklin both loved and hated the desert. It was, he knew, his implacable enemy, but there was something about it that made him feel more alive, something like the western sky at night and the sea at any time.

Buck fidgeted and Rocklin came out of his musings. It was time to do something about the two hardcases that had been on his trail ever since he had left the train in Las Vegas. He certainly couldn't have them following him into the valley. It would handicap him, for one thing. For another, it would put him in great danger to have anyone getting curious about what he was up to.

He spotted them easily, five, six miles back, taking their time, and he wondered if they could possibly know where he was headed. No, no chance. Only one man knew that, and he was in Chicago. Still, in ten days of riding they had never seemed too worried about losing his trail. On the other hand, there were not too many places a man could be going in this direction. Rocklin knew they were following him because a couple of days out of Las Vegas he had started testing them — slowing down, speeding up, making a daytime camp unexpectedly, leaving them to decide whether to go ahead or hang back—it was an automatic precaution for a man in Rocklin's line of work.

He had spent the night at the stage stop partly just to see what they would do. They skirted it, camped among some big rocks nearby and started dogging him again in the morning, five or six miles back. Now why would a couple of drifters avoid a stage stop where there might be some rotgut whisky? Why pass up a chance for a hot meal, a steak, some beans and passable sourdough and even some preserves made from cactus pears? Could it be they were flat broke?

Well, it made no difference now. And the night at the stage stop had been enjoyable. The old man who ran it welcomed company and liked to talk. He was called Whiskers, claimed he didn't remember his last name. He knew how the stage stop had gotten its name, though—Old Lady Wells. It seems that in the early days a settler's wagon ran out of water and the people were about to die. They had pulled up on the shady side of a mountain-high pile of rocks and everyone but a sick old lady had started circling around scouting for signs of a seep that was supposed to be in the area. Suddenly the old lady sat up in the wagon and announced that she smelled water. Then she climbed down and walked in among the rocks for about 50 yards and found a small depression that was lined with caked and cracked mud. It was a good story and the old man told it well. He also talked about the Sweetwater, but not before feeling Rocklin out.

"Ridin' far?"

"Down from Las Vegas," Rocklin told him.

"Fair piece," the old man commented, and then waited.

Rocklin knew the rules well. Conversations about people's business had to start very tentatively in this country. But to hear something, a man sometimes had to say something, and hearing things was an important, a crucial, part of Rocklin's stock in trade.

"Probably won't go much farther than Sweetwater."

Any reply that contains information is an invitation for further talk. The old man eyed Rocklin a minute. "Cattleman?" he asked, although he knew just by looking at him that Rocklin wasn't.

"Nope."

"More coffee?" the old man asked.

"Be obliged. Sure doesn't taste like trail coffee."

The old man took the compliment as offered and afterward sat awhile in silence.

"Trouble in the Sweetwater," he said.

"Oh? What kind of trouble?"

"Greed. Murder. The usual kind, wherever you find the human critter."

"Murder? That's a pretty flat statement."

"Murder."

"Over what?"

"Land. Water. Cattle. Just like the world's first killin'. See, things ain't changed since Cain and Abel." The old man chuckled without humor. "Hear the governor of the territory is sendin' a special agent down to look into it."

Rocklin was startled. The garrulous old fool was gazing at him blandly. A special agent from Santa Fe? It could be a complication. The old man had to be headed off.

"A special agent? Is that the sort of thing that is generally known?"

"Not generally. But it's known."

"Hm. Who is the main problem? Is he known?"

"Depends on who you're talkin' to. Some say a man named MacCrue and some say a man named Belsher. Hendryx, one of the early ranchers down in the south valley, thinks it's Belsher."

"Does he have a reason?"

"Belsher's new. Bought the old Star ranch from Red Dunbar's heirs. Heard of Dunbar?"

"Nope. It's my first time down this way."

"Apache-fightin' hellraiser. Tamed this country. Gun and rope. Hanged anyone who so much as looked at one of his cows. Anyway, place kinda ran down after he died, and finally Belsher showed up. Plenty of money. Probably

10

some Eastern money."

"Is that unusual?"

"Oh no. Gettin' to be purty common, I guess. Hear there's even some furrin' money around. Next thing, you'll see wire."

Again Rocklin was startled. But he was a careful man, in no hurry. He was doing a job and kept his feelings to himself. He merely nodded. He was thinking of something he had seen on a railroad flat car in Las Vegas after he had unloaded Buck and settled him down.

Buck had acted up — tossed his head against the bit, skittered and scolded — just to let him know how he felt about riding on trains, so a little soft talk and sugar was called for. Then Rocklin had noticed the huge load, maybe a hundred spools of barbed wire, each spool weighing close to a thousand pounds. Who was it for? It must be some brand out of Jackson, a town about fifty miles west of Sweetwater that was the last stop on the single freight line serving the area. What was the brand? Yes, the Lazy D.

"It will all change, I suspect, and sooner than we think," Rocklin said.

"Yep," the old man said, "but I'll be dead, and glad of it."

Rocklin was thinking about a way to get off the subject. So far the old man hadn't told him anything he didn't already know. But the re-mark about wire was helpful. It gave Rocklin

11

an idea.

"And then there's Belsher's brand," Whiskers said.

Rocklin yawned. "Brand?"

"The Double B. That's Belsher's brand. It's downright amazin' how easy it is to make a Double B out of a Lazy H."

"The Hendryx brand, I take it," Rocklin said.

"You guessed it?"

Rocklin laughed. "You know, Whiskers, I haven't heard such loose talk since I left the train. If I ever have anything to report from around here, remind me to ride to Jackson. I wouldn't want a pouch with any of my mail in it to come anywhere near this stage stop."

The old man sulked for a minute, pretending to be offended. He was studying Rocklin's clothes.

Rocklin's hat, on the table, was one of the new Stetsons, cream-colored, with a smaller brim and crown than a cowhand's. And his pants, of a tough, tightly woven corduroy material, and matching vest and light shirt did not come off the shelf at some railroad town or cow-town trading post. An expensive, long-wearing get-up, good for traveling and good for business. Then the old man was eyeing Rocklin's heavy, flat-heeled boots.

"What would you be reportin'?" Ain't much minin' around here," he said mildly.

Rocklin thought about that a minute. He was pleased that the canny old man had brought it up. "Might be," he said.

The old man snorted. "It's been tried, plenty of times. Besides, you don't look like no prospector I ever saw." It was a direct approach, and Rocklin welcomed it.

"I am, though. That's exactly what I am, in a way. As you have observed, times are changing."

"Don't matter how much they change, there's still no gold anywhere around here, and I ought to know."

"Looked it over, have you?"

"From top to bottom."

"Well, Whiskers, there are other things besides gold. Quite a few things. There's silver . . ."

"Ain't no silver either."

"Maybe not. But what about copper? Lead and zinc? Iron ore? Even coal? A few hundred miles west of here, a man found a huge hill, almost a mountain, of iron ore. He's rich. At least the company that sent him out is rich, and if the man is smart, he got his share."

"How'd he find it? You don't go scratchin' around with a pick for iron ore."

"Well, no. It can help. But the modern prospector is part mining engineer and part geologist . . . that's a man who has studied—"

"I know what it is," the old man yelped, his

13

feelings hurt.

"And you've prospected. Hell, you know how it is. It's mostly experience and good hunches. But some of it is knowing about the lay of the land, the way the hills stick out of the ground, the layers of rock on the face of a cliff, the color of the soil . . ."

"The taste of the water?"

"Sometimes even that helps, yes."

"What do you think you'll find?"

"Don't know. But whatever it is, it won't create any sensation, or any sudden rush. It will be the sort of thing the big companies want. I mean companies that have the money and equipment to dig enough of it to make it pay." Rocklin paused, chuckling, "So actually, you can talk about it all you want."

The old man practically cackled. "And don't think I won't," he said. "More coffee?"

"No thanks. I think I'll bunk down pretty soon."

"Another cup won't hurt you. And I don't get to talk a lot, usually."

Rocklin was glad he had stayed overnight with the old man. His ostensible business in the valley would quickly get around, and now all he had to do was lay the right groundwork with the ranchers and he could wander about pretty much as he pleased. It was a lucky stop,

14

and a little luck was always welcome.

But luck wouldn't take care of his two shadows. He decided to make camp early, off the trail, far enough to be inconspicuous but not so far that the men couldn't smell his fire. He had to find out about them. They were probably just what they had seemed when he first saw them, drifters, predators, as dirty and smelly and useless as men could get, men who would cut anybody's throat for a drink, but not if there was the slightest chance that the killing would raise a stink or that they would ever be found out. They would want to toy with their victim first, partly for the cruel satisfaction of it and partly to find out who and what he was.

Rocklin had taken their measure, casually, in Las Vegas, and after he had discovered them on his trail, had found a vantage point where he couldn't be seen and had studied them carefully with his field glasses.

He made up his mind. He would make camp, eat, drink coffee and wait for them to walk in on him.

Chapter 2

The town of Sweetwater, New Mexico Territory, lay about halfway down the valley on flatland just below the western slope of the mountain range, and anybody who had spent much time in the West could read its history plainly, if he cared to look. First of all, it was not situated on the best land around, far from it. The best land was kept for the cattle. Also, the town had once burned, as Western towns often did, and the two remaining buildings from the old town were a general store and a saloon. They both showed old, black scars from the fire and both had been enlarged, the newer portions now looking almost as weatherbeaten as the older. Then they had been painted, in front, just so they could keep up appearances with the new buildings going up around them.

Then, in gradual stages, came a livery stable, a feed and grain store, a smithy, an express office and stage stop, a grandiose two-story hotel with twelve rooms on the second floor and a lobby, dining room and kitchen on the first. A small bank followed, along with the few scattered homes of the townspeople. And then a jail, twelve feet long and six feet wide inside, fairly commodious as cow-town jails went, with rock walls two feet thick. It had a door that any man over five-foot-ten would have to stoop to get through, and a window eighteen inches square with bars an inch and a half thick. There was no bunk and the floor was dirt.

Next came a small church, a one-room school, and some shrubs and trees. The main trading establishments in town had acquired, a short stretch at a time, wooden sidewalks; and this refinement, along with the patches of green and the whitewashed exteriors and fences of the better-kept homes, the church and the school, made Sweetwater a real town—population 56, give or take a few, and elevation about 3,000 feet.

At about the time that Rocklin was inviting his would-be murderers to have some coffee, six men were sitting in the smoky, highly charged atmosphere of the town saloon. The owner of the place had vanished — he knew the men were good for whatever they drank — and anyone else who wandered in was told the saloon was closed for a meeting. One of the men, a gnarled old fighter with white hair, had his hand on his gun and was glaring at a younger man, almost a youth except for his hard and wiry frame and his ferocious eyes.

"Go ahead and draw," white hair said.

The young man's face was tight, and deep red under the brown skin. He was almost shaking with his effort at control. "I didn't reckon I'd need a gun at such a friendly meeting," he said.

"Damn it Hendryx, no one needs a gun," Ed Belsher said to the older man. "Now can you see why I suggested we all leave them on the bar."

"I don't take my gun off for anyone," white hair said.

"That's smart," the younger man said. "You may need it at any time if you keep calling me a cow thief."

Belsher turned to the younger man. "And that's just what I mean, MacCrue. He didn't call you a cow thief."

"Same as."

"No, it isn't the same as. Now we all talked this out before we started. We're in a bad situation here, and we've got to get together or we'll have this valley overrun with authority of one kind or another. We all know there are strong feelings here, even suspicions, but we have to lay it all out on the table just the same. And if somebody's going to be insulted every time anybody says anything, we'll never get anywhere."

"I only remarked that MacCrue hasn't lost many cattle," Hendryx said.

"And I only remarked that if you're accusing me of rustling, you're a liar," MacCrue shot back.

Other men spoke up, some taking sides and some trying to pour oil on troubled waters.

"Now that's enough," Belsher shouted. "He didn't say you was a rustler, MacCrue."

"And I didn't say he was a liar, necessarily."

A rancher named Brennan spoke up. "Then what did you say? Let's hear it." And then as others started to speak, Brennan raised his voice. "And one at a time. I can't stay here all night."

Purley White spoke up. "Brennan's right. So is Belsher. If this is going to do any good at all, which I doubt, the cards have to be on the table."

"Why do you doubt it?" Belsher asked mildly.

"Wait a minute," Brennan said. "We'll get to that. First MacCrue. What about it Mac-Crue?"

"What about what?"

Brennan looked disgusted. White said, "I'm leaving."

"All right," MacCrue said. "All right." He stopped and took a swallow of whisky, his third, although everyone present knew he wasn't a drinker. He looked around the saloon at each man in turn and then said, "There isn't a man here I could consider a friend." He ignored the burst of comments and pressed on. "I was just a lad when my folks came to the valley and bought the section of land where I live. It was all they could afford. When they died in the big raid in '70, I was only fifteen years old, just about the age my brother is now. But I kept it. And I hung on to it. By myself."

"You were offered help," Hendryx said.

"I was offered a price."

"You were offered help, too. I myself—"

"All right! I said I was just a lad. I thought you'd try to take advantage of me. And I know I wasn't very sociable, but it's

21

the way I grew up." He brushed it away impatiently. "But that's not the main thing, and you all know it.

"When Dunbar died I could have bought his ranch. I had a little money and my own place free and clear. But all of you squeezed me out. Why?"

There was silence for a couple of minutes. Men poured drinks.

"Well?" MacCrue said.

Brennan spoke up. "Son, Dunbar's four sections were right across the headwaters of Sweetwater Creek. And we didn't trust you."

"But Belsher came in, a newcomer you didn't even know. Do you trust Belsher?"

"That's a damn good question," Hendryx said. It was his normal tone, but it was deep and raspy and came from his belly. All the men but Belsher turned to look at him. Purley White said, "Let it wait Jen. Your turn'll come. Besides we all know what you think."

Brennan turned back to MacCrue and asked, "What can you say about the fact that Belsher has lost at least a couple of hundred head and you haven't lost any?"

MacCrue took a minute to bring himself under control again. All the men could see what it cost him to talk, and one or two were beginning to feel some sympathy.

22

"Does it mean all that much? In the first place I don't have many head. In the second place, I'm boxed in back in that canyon where a coyote couldn't come in without being seen, and in the third place, Jimmy and I have been trading off watch at the head of that canyon every night, all night, for six months."

The men in the room just stared at him. Except Rusty Mack. Rusty hadn't said a word all evening. Now he laughed. "You truly ain't very sociable, are you son?"

Ed Belsher gazed at MacCrue briefly and asked, "And what do you do, let your stock out into the valley in the daytime for water and round them up again at night?"

"I've got water," MacCrue said. And then he stopped talking. It was plain to everyone in the room.

"A well, sure, but do you mean your herd's so small you can water 'em from a well?"

The men waited. Then Belsher pressed a little harder. "Would you mind if a couple of us rode up and visited a spell?"

The men still waited.

Alex MacCrue stood up. "I'll shoot any man who rides into my canyon." He started for the door.

"MacCrue!" It was Hendryx's deep and

commanding voice. "You're a damn fool if you leave it like this."

"I'm not leaving it any way. It's already what it is. Four men, your men and Belsher's men have died in a shootout right where you're sitting. Six men from six different outfits have been shot from ambush on the open range. A deputy from Jackson was bushwhacked on the way over here. Your foreman, Hendryx, one of the most respected men in the valley, with a wife and two children, was shot out of his saddle on his way to town. And every one of you have hired gunmen. All right. You froze me out once and you'll leave me alone now."

MacCrue looked straight at Belsher. "And all of you were supposed to leave your men home tonight, but I saw the Laredo Kid ride in just ahead of me. If I don't make it home, you know who to ask about it."

There was silence in the room after MacCrue left. Belsher's face was a study. It was almost pale, but its expression was close to a tolerant smile.

"He's an impossible kid to like," Hendryx said. "But I'd bet my bottom dollar that he never told a lie in his life."

"I told the Kid to stay home," Belsher said offhandedly. "But he's got a girl in town.

24

And just the same, I think we should manage somehow to get a look at MacCrue's canyon."

Chapter 3

Rocklin heard the two men coming a mile off.

The sun had just disappeared below the tops of the mountains but its rays were still touching the crags of a smaller range far to the east, turning them a golden brown. An uncanny silence seemed to move across the desert with the shadows, and in that silence, far down the rocky trail, Rocklin could hear the unmistakable crunch of hooves, and even the occasional sound of a voice. It puzzled him that two men riding along intent on robbery and murder could be so indifferent to what their victim might be thinking. He wondered again if they could know who he was, or—a new thought—if they thought he was the rumored special deputy from Santa Fe. But in that case, why would they have been waiting in Las Vegas to pick up his trail? No.

Then he thought about Joe Ferrigan. Bannister had mentioned Ferrigan in Chicago after he had laid the problem out for Rocklin in his usual thorough way, with maps of the Sweetwater area, the different brands in the valley, the names of the ranchers and as much of their history as he knew, and even the spots, marked roughly on the map, where men had been bushwhacked. Rocklin had asked, "How many people in the valley?"

"It varies, of course," Bannister had said. "Roundup isn't typical. I'd say roughly twenty-five hundred, usually. But they are spread out. Three hundred square miles, you know. Ranchers, cowhands, a few farms, townspeople."

"You haven't mentioned how the Cattlemen's Association happened to catch on to the situation," Rocklin had said.

"A letter. Unsigned."

Rocklin eyed him for a moment. Bannister was hard to read, which, Rocklin supposed, was as it should be, since he was the top trouble-shooter for the association.

"No guess as to who sent it?"

"No."

"So it could be a straightforward request for help, or some kind of trick."

"Yes."

28

"Do you still have the letter?"

Bannister opened a drawer, took out a creased and travel-worn sheet of paper with scrawled printing on it and handed it to Rocklin. "It won't tell you much," he said. And he was right. It merely said there was rustling and murder in the valley and asked for help.

Rocklin waited. He knew there was more, and he knew that he probably wasn't going to like it; it wasn't like Bannister to stall. Bannister shifted in his chair. It wasn't like him to be uneasy, either. Rocklin decided he needed prodding. "It's in the middle of nowhere. The problem can't be all that complicated. Why me?"

Bannister shifted in his chair again. Finally he said, "We sent Joe Ferrigan. Do you know Joe?"

"I've met him. And?"

"And nothing." Rocklin waited. "I mean, he got off the train at Las Cruces, bought a horse, took the two-day ride to Jackson — that's the county seat and the nearest major town to the valley — spent a couple of days there and rode out. That's all we know. As far as we know, no one has seen or heard from him since." He looked blankly at Rocklin. "So maybe the problem is more complicated than we thought."

29

Rocklin sat mulling this new information, and Bannister tried to read some slight expression on his face. Rocklin didn't like ground that had been tramped over — and Bannister knew it — but he didn't rant and he didn't even cuss a little. He might have been scanning a poker hand before deciding to fold. "So somebody's been alerted," he said.

"Might have been," Bannister said. "We don't know. Anything could have happened. You know that."

"But we have to assume somebody's been alerted."

"Obviously."

Again Rocklin took his time; this new information changed things considerably. Finally he said, "It will cost you."

Bannister shrugged with his shoulders and his hands. "You should have some reason for going down there," he said.

"I do have. I've arranged a legitimate trip."

"Will you try to pick up Ferrigan's trail?"

"Absolutely not. I'll go in the long way, from the north." He saw the doubt in Bannister's raised eyebrows. "I'll have a believable reason for wanting to look the country over."

So whoever was causing the trouble in Sweetwater Valley might have had eyes and ears in Jackson, Rocklin thought, but it would certainly be stretching it to assume he had people watching every train stop from Santa Fe to El Paso—especially bunglers like the two men approaching his camp.

Buck was perking his ears and snorting. "I hear them, boy," Rocklin soothed. "Just settle down and let me handle it."

He made a small fire around a flat rock with ironwood, hard old chunks of dead chaparral that burn long and hot, and took a coffee pot, some jerky and a can of beans from his roll. He took two heavy hunting knives and a gun, one of the new double action Colt .38s, from his saddle bags. He arranged a rock seat, with his back to the direction of the men's approach, and stashed his weapons under his saddle on the ground next to his seat where he could reach them with a minimum of fuss.

Then he stood for a minute studying the arrangement. Finally, he decided to put the gun back in the saddlebags and hang them on the broken stump of a nearby branch. He stuck one of the knives into a chunk of wood by the fire and concealed the other under his coat.

He felt easier about the risk of such an arrangement, since the men were making no effort whatever to sneak up on him. And if they got the idea that he was just another unwary Western traveler, they might decide to sit awhile and have a cup of coffee before they killed him. If his luck held he would be able to use the knives. A shot at this time of the evening from this desert altitude might be heard for ten miles, and with the tense situation in the Sweetwater, might cause someone to wonder. He settled himself to eat and wait.

They left their horses a few yards back and walked straight into his camp without saying a word.

Rocklin felt better. No one with friendly intentions would approach a strange camp that way. They would let themselves be known, ride in when invited and step down when invited.

They could have been twins. Same scruffy beards, same dirty hats with holes at the front of the crease, same filthy bandannas and shirts, same pants and chaps with so much accumulated grime that they could have stood by themselves, and same boots, down at the heels and curling up at the toes. Same old hardware in the same old worn holsters. And the same sour look stamped permanently on their brutish faces.

"Smelled coffee," one of them said.

"Find a seat," Rocklin said. "There's plenty. Made extra when I heard you coming."

They glanced at each other, looked more closely at Rocklin and then lifted their hats, ran hands over their heads and settled their hats. Same gestures too. Only one of them was nearly bald. Rocklin remembered seeing their faces on wanted posters some time ago and he knew their names. He offered them a couple of cans to drink from and some jerky and they settled down.

"Who's paying you?" Rocklin asked.

They stared. "What?" Baldy said.

"Who sent you after me?"

They considered this. "You on the run?" Baldy asked.

"No. Not exactly."

The other one continued to stare, his mouth partly open. Rocklin wondered if he was playing with a full deck. Well, he'd gotten his answer, anyway. No chance that the men knew who he was.

"It's interesting, the people you meet on the trail," Rocklin said in a conversational tone. "Sometimes you can tell exactly what a person is just by looking at him. Other times you can't be sure. I'd think that's one of the things that could make crime so risky. There's always the danger that you could pick the wrong victim."

The men looked at each other again, and then back at Rocklin. Their expressions had changed. The silent one was looking a little wary, and baldy was sneering, as though he felt distrust and contempt for a man who talked too much and too well.

"And just who might you be," baldy asked. The other man glanced at his partner in surprise, but baldy was busy sizing up Rocklin, eyeing his clothes, studying his horse, noticing the knife in the wood.

"Just a drifter," Rocklin said, a patent lie. "Noticed you two back in Las Vegas, and wondered about you. Would you like a can of beans? I have some left, and I'll be where I'm going tomorrow."

Baldy's grin was more like a sneer. "And just what did you wonder about us?"

"Oh, where you'd been; where you were going. You were obviously down on your luck, and had been for a while. And you were obviously looking around for something, and it wasn't work. Been in prison?"

The dummy was looking sour and his hand edged to his gun and rested there.

"Go ahead, run off at the mouth," baldy said, and it wasn't necessary for him to add: while you have the chance.

"And then you both acted as though everybody around you was blind." Rocklin said. "People looked at you, gave you a second look, and put some distance between you and

34

them. They knew exactly what kind of men you were and what you were looking for." Baldy took out his gun. "And the thing was," Rocklin said, with not the slightest change of tone, "You seemed completely unaware, as though you thought you were invisible or something."

Baldy got up and turned Rocklin's saddle over with his toe. "Where's your gun?" he said.

"It's what made me wonder if you had been out of circulation for a while." Rocklin said.

"Look in his saddlebags," baldy told his partner, and sat back down. "You just talk to hear your head rattle, don't you?" he said to Rocklin. "Well go ahead. Pretty soon you won't have a head because I'm going to blow it off."

The other man took Rocklin's gun from the saddlebags, looked at it curiously and tossed it to baldy. Baldy looked it over, glanced at Rocklin contemptuously and said, "What do you kill with it, rattlesnakes?"

"It's the new double action .38. And it's plenty powerful enough for what I need to kill."

Baldy cocked his gun.

"What's this?" the dummy asked, much to Rocklin's astonishment. The man tossed a heavy book to baldy.

"Mining and miner—al . . ."

"Mining and mineralogy," Rocklin said. "It's one of the tools of my trade." Baldy threw it in the fire.

"Here's another one," The man tossed a small, leather-bound volume to baldy and turned back to the bags.

"Emerson," baldy said. He stared at Rocklin with about as mean a look as Rocklin had ever seen. Then he put his gun down, grabbed the pages of the book and ripped. In that instant, Rocklin hurled a knife. It buried itself in the side of baldy's throat just under his chin. The man grabbed the handle with both hands, stared at Rocklin in utter disbelief, then with the realization that he was dead. As he was crumpling sideways, some sound or movement warned the other man. He whirled, pulling his gun, just as Rocklin's other knife went in to the hilt just below his left breast.

Rocklin quickly doused and scatted his fire, hoping it had not by any chance been spotted in the growing dark. He scouted around until he found a ravine among the rocks, not very deep but deep enough, then he took the two men's guns and some of their .45 ammunition, which would fit his rifle as well as their guns, and carried the bodies to the ravine and

Chapter 4

Alex MacCrue and his kid brother, Jimmy, had just finished loading supplies into their wagon and were tying them down when Alex saw Jenny Lee come out of the hotel dining room with Laredo. Laredo, in his usual flamboyant get-up, was being overly polite, bowing her out the door with a wide grin, and Jenny was laughing at him. When she saw Alex watching her with a scowl she raised her eyebrows at him and started chatting gaily with the Kid.

The Kid was turning all his charm on Jenny and didn't see MacCrue until he was abreast of him, then he stopped, his face darkening. He left Jenny's side and walked to the edge of the boardwalk to confront MacCrue.

"I hear you've been intimatin' that I'm a bushwhacker," he said.

MacCrue ignored him, turning to Jenny. "It

39

doesn't look good for a schoolteacher to be too friendly with a hired gunslinger," he said.

Jenny blushed but held his eyes. "Does that concern you?"

The Kid stepped down off the walk. "Did you hear what I said?"

MacCrue was still looking at Jenny, and showing a little color himself. "It might," he said. Jenny raised her brows at him again. It was a trick she had that was both attractive and infuriating. "And how, pray?" she said.

The Kid jerked MacCrue's arm. "Why don't you wear a gun?" he demanded.

MacCrue eyed him with insulting indifference. "It's not polite for a man to start a fight when he's with a lady," he said. "It just isn't fitting." He turned back to Jenny. "You'd best go home."

"I'll thank you to . . ."

The Kid jerked MacCrue's arm again. "Did you hear what I—"

MacCrue spun around and knocked him cold. Then he stepped up onto the walk, facing Jenny. "You'd best get some sense," he said. "People are watching. Would you like for me to walk along with you?"

Jenny stared at him, speechless, then turned and walked away.

Alex and Jimmy were about a mile out of

town when they heard a rider coming up behind them at an easy canter.

"Don't look back," Alex said, as Jimmy started to turn. "It might be the Laredo Kid. Just ease the rifle out."

The rider drew abreast of the wagon, slowed down, and much to Alex's surprise said, "Mornin' MacCrue." It was Rusty Mack.

Alex slowed his team down a bit, nodded briefly and said, "Mornin'." He remembered that Rusty had had little to say at the meeting the night before, and he also remembered the man's laugh when he told him and the others about his unneighborly night watch.

"Hi son." Jimmy looked at the man, grinned, and said "Hi."

"Saw what happened back there," Rusty told Alex. "And I've gotta say, young man, that you have a mighty unusual style of courtin'."

Alex was startled. He felt the blood in his face and it irritated him, he felt it was the reaction of a child. "How does it concern you?" he said.

"Oh now, now." Rusty chuckled. "Just passin' a remark. Mind if I ride up with you to the fork?"

Alex pulled up. "Isn't it out of your way?" he said, not very cordially.

"Not much." The man dismounted and tied his horse to the back of the wagon. Jimmy swung around into the wagon bed and settled down, and the man thanked him and took his seat.

"Pretty hard life out here for a woman," he said. "They don't get to do much socializing. Always something to do. Hard. And you know, I reckon the women who have it hardest of all are the ones married to grouchy men with no sense of humor."

Alex was dumb with astonishment. What was this talky old man's point?

"Buried two wives, myself, and I know."

Alex didn't know what to say. They rode awhile in silence. Finally Alex said, "I remember your place. I was down that way a couple of times with my father."

"He was a good man, your father. Stiff-necked as hell, but absolutely straight." He twisted around in the wagon seat to look at Jimmy. "You're Jimmy, is that right?"

"Yessir."

"I'm Rusty Mack."

"How 'do, sir."

Rusty turned back to Alex. "Good. You taught him to talk like a little man. Never had any younguns myself."

Again Alex was put off by the direct and personal manner of the man. He didn't know how to reply and he wondered if it was a lack in himself. He was remembering the man's house, all timbers and adobe. It seemed huge, but maybe that was just because he had been a boy. "Being way down there, you must know everything that comes and goes in this valley," he said.

"Yup. And if you're wondering about any little bunches of stray cows, I dinna ken." He chuckled at Alex's surprise. "Your daddy used to say that. We joined up on a couple of trail drives.

"Nope. Criss-crossed that end of the valley ten times. Course all the drives start down that way. No way of telling. None at all. Personally, I think the stock's still right here somewhere."

"Not on my place," Alex said.

"Probably not. Last night after you left, Hendryx reckoned you never told a lie in your life. And me? I'd be hornswoggled if your daddy ever raised a thief."

Alex tried to control his flush, and thought he did pretty well. "They didn't go away and hide all by themselves," he said.

"Nope." Silence, then: "I'm too tired for all this. I hate it. I've fought my fights, and I just want to . . . men I've rode with for years . . ." He sighed. "Well, I'm not going into it blind. I've smelled this kind of trouble before, and it always had to do with the hunger for land, and more land.

"It started with that damn Homestead Act, of course."

"You think squatters are causing the trouble?" Alex asked, surprised.

43

"No. Oh no. I've had a couple of 'em down next to me. No trouble. Couldn't make it, of course. Sold a bill of goods by the government and some railroad lookin' to drum up future business, and came down here on a shoestring, not even enough to get 'em through one year. Bought 'em out eventually. Gave 'em a fair price for their quarter sections. One of 'em supportin' his family by clerkin' in a store over in Jackson. Other went back East. Shoulda never left.

"Nope. It was the Act itself. Opened up a can of worms. You can hear of it happening already. Big outfits ending up with everything. Wire. No more open range. And I just know it's happening right here in my valley. I can smell it. And I won't go into it blind.

"You're smart to stay out of it, son. Stick to your guns."

Alex was remembering the bitter days after his parents were killed. "You came up to my place a couple of times after the trouble," he said.

Rusty chuckled. "Talk about stiff-necked. You were going to show the world, you were. Well, guess I'll get off here."

When he had mounted, he touched his hat in a kind of salute and said, "Thanks for the ride. Oh. And look out for that Laredo. He'll be out to kill you now, and he won't care which way you're facin'."

Alex was quiet for a long time as the steady slow trot of the big horses pounded off the miles. Jimmy was quiet too, but he kept glancing sideways at his brother. Finally, he said, "Is that man with the fancy guns really going to try to kill you?"

Alex started. "What? Oh. Trying and doing are two different things. Don't you go worrying about that, now." He pulled lightly on the reins to let the team walk awhile.

"What does stiff-necked mean?" Jimmy asked.

"I don't know, I guess it means set in your ways, maybe. Or stubborn."

Jimmy thought that over. "Is it an insult?"

"I don't reckon so. It would depend on the way it was said, I guess."

"You look like you're mad," Jimmy said.

Alex stared at the boy. "Well, I'm not." Jimmy was silenced for a while, and Alex asked him, "Do I look like that a lot? I mean like I'm mad?" He was thinking about his father, who was a serious man and a hard taskmaster.

"I reckon not," Jimmy said, clearly trying not to be hurtful.

Alex felt a sudden inexplicable emotion that made him want to put his arm around his brother. His thoughtful scowl deepened and he wondered what was happening to him. "You're a good brother," he said. "I couldn't get along without you." Jimmy flushed and looked down at his hands. Remembering his father's quick color when he was angered, Alex wondered if it was some sort of MacCrue trait. His mother didn't show her feelings like that . . . always even-tempered, even though she did go after dirt like she was after the devil himself.

As he thought of his father and mother, Alex MacCrue consciously tried to soften his expression, and to his own astonishment he found himself wondering if they had been happy together. It was damn foolishness. Then he thought of Jenny Lee.

"Are you a-courtin' Miss Lee?" Jimmy asked.

It fair took Alex's breath away. They seemed to be thinking at the same level and talking like they had never talked before. Jimmy was watching him with his upward sideways look. Alex almost smiled. "Hmph. Not very well, I guess." Then he realized that "Miss Lee" was Jimmy's teacher, and that the boy probably knew a lot more about her than he did. "Do you like her?"

"Yes. She's pretty," Jimmy said, getting down to basics. Alex looked at him and realized that he was just a year younger than he, Alex, had been when he took over the man-size job of hanging on to the ranch. He actually grinned.

"She laughs a lot," Jimmy said.

"Laughs?"

"Well, you know, like when one of the boys is trying to put something over on her. She just sort of laughs him out of it without shamin' him."

"Is she stern sometimes?"

"Oh. Well, you know. She's . . . well, she makes you work. But it's not so bad because you kinda want to work. For her, I mean. See? Sometimes, if you do really well, she pays you a compliment." Jimmy bit his lip.

Alex was thoughtful. "I see," he said.

"But that ain't . . . that's not so good, see. Because then the other boys get on you . . . you know, call you teacher's pet and that, and you have to beat 'em up."

Alex almost laughed. He reached over and patted his brother on the shoulder. Jimmy gave a deep sigh and looked down at his hands. Alex wondered if the expression on the lad's face was happiness. He wondered about Jenny Lee. He pictured Jenny Lee laughing. He wondered if he could learn how to dance.

Chapter 5

Rocklin took the better part of two weeks scouting Sweetwater Valley. He started high in the timber on the west side and zigzagged up and down, moving carefully and cautiously, rarely going above or below the timberlines, and then only when the terrain offered good cover, and always making a cold camp at night. Occasionally he stopped during the day when he found a good vantage point with nothing around him but sheltering rocks and the sky, and built a small fire for hot coffee and beans. He stopped and listened. From a vantage point he would study the terrain for hours using his glasses, taking care to mark the position of the sun, mindful of reflection.

He was never in a hurry, and before he was through he knew more about the valley than people who had lived there all their lives. He knew where the oak and pine and spruce and juniper were, and he knew more—the alluvial deposits, the flat layers of sedimentary rock, the steep layers of folded rocks, some porous sandstone, some granite. He knew the watershed, where it was green and full, gradually feeding the thirsty valley, and where it had burned off years ago, making the land below susceptible to flash floods. He knew too, because it was part of his job, that there were few recoverable minerals. Some potash at the extreme southern end of the western foothills and maybe, he thought, some oil. He intended to look into that when he had the chance.

It had been a careful and comprehensive survey—and there had been only one hitch. Three renegade Indians had picked up his trail as he approached the southern end of the western mountains, and it had taken the better part of four days to finally shake them.

Buck, with a restless movement and a snort, had warned him of the beginning of the trouble. Rocklin had drunk the last of some cold coffee and had just started to settle down for the night when he heard Buck's signal. He had quickly gathered a few pieces of wood, wrapped his bedroll around them and left them near his saddle. Then he moved into the shadows, closer to Buck, and settled down between two large rocks with a tree at his back.

He could hear nothing but the normal night-time rustle of the woods, but he knew something was around because Buck remained skittish and had to be quieted. The first silent figure passed almost within arm's length of him before he knew it was there, and Rocklin realized it was an Indian. He let the man go by, not wanting to alert others who might be nearby with the sounds of a scuffle. The Indian crept toward the camp and then stopped, waiting. Then there must have been some sort of signal, because he and two others rushed Rocklin's bedroll from three different directions.

Rocklin moved swiftly, aware that it would take only an instant for the Indians to realize they had attacked a decoy, and to know that someone was out there in the darkness watching. He was almost on top of them before they had gotten over their surprise and started to move.

A quick blow to the neck brought one of the men down as though he had been pole-axed, and the other two, glancing back and seeing that Rocklin was unarmed, stopped and turned to face him. It was just what Rocklin wanted. The men had knives and they were moving slowly toward him from different directions, but both were in his field of sight and he hoped that his fighting tactics would catch them completely by surprise. He didn't especially want to kill the men. It could cause him endless trouble and interfere with the job he had to do. But he did want to discourage them if possible.

Rocklin rushed first, picking the man nearest him. He parried a murderous knife thrust, levered the man up, feeling the arm bone pop out of the shoulder socket, and threw him into the other rushing Indian. Before the other Indian recovered enough to know from which direction Rocklin was coming, he was unconscious.

Rocklin set about tidying up. He dragged the three men together and tied them securely. When he had immobilized the one with the dislocated shoulder, he took a firm hold on his arm. The man pulled back involuntarily, glaring hatred at Rocklin.

"Sit still old woman," Rocklin snapped at him in Apache. The astonished man sat still. Taking great care, Rocklin manipulated the arm bone back into its shoulder socket. He double checked his knots, making sure that it would take the men hours to work free, then sat and thought, waiting for the other men to come to.

It was highly unlikely that any stray Indians were involved in the rustling in Sweetwater Valley. They couldn't sell the cattle unless they drove them to Mexico, which they would not do, and they wouldn't steal them to eat. Indians did not particularly like beef and preferred horse meat. Besides, Rocklin knew there had been no real trouble with the Apaches in this part of the territory for several years, and most of them lived on a small reservation near Jackson and on the much larger Mescalero reservation farther north. If a few of them occasionally left the reservations and wandered the mountains looking for game, nobody minded—as long as they caused no trouble. It was not like the situation in Arizona Territory, where Geronimo still raided from time to time from his hideout in Mexico's Sierra Madre. Rocklin had little doubt that the three men who had tried to jump him just wanted his horse and his weapons. They had only carried knives.

At first light Rocklin scouted the vicinity of the camp and brought in the Indians' ponies. Two of them were pintos, and Rocklin knew that most Apaches looked on pintos as inferior mounts. The third horse, however, was a sorrel, and its hooves showed signs of shoes, although there was no brand.

The Indians saw Rocklin examining the sorrel, as he had intended they should. He gave them a hard look and, unnecessarily, checked the loads in his revolver and rifle. He saw them stop working at their bonds and stiffen momentarily. When he was ready to leave he turned to them and said, "Don't follow me. Much trouble." Three pairs of eyes looked through him, and he knew the men would kill him if they happened on the slightest opportunity. Otherwise, he thought, they would probably leave him alone.

Three days later they almost had the opportunity. Rocklin was scouting the southern tip of the mountains where they turned into piles of rocks and dwindled into the vast southern desert. He was just emerging from a small canyon when the Indians rode around the edge of a crag not much more than a mile away. Buck stopped instantly and edged slowly back into another small opening in the cliff-like rocks. There were six of them. Rocklin thought one of the horses looked like the sorrel, but he couldn't be sure. He faded deeper into the deep cleft and took out his glasses. It was the sorrel, and there were the three men who had tried to rob him. If they kept riding in the direction they were headed, they would easily spot Rocklin's trail—and know that it was fresh. They only had knives, but at six to one they might decide it was worth the risk and try to surprise him if they thought he was boxed in.

They were coming closer. Rocklin didn't see how they could miss him now, and he resigned himself to a shooting war. But suddenly the Indians veered away from the rocks and into the flat desert. He watched them until they disappeared over the horizon, then he turned and looked around him. Farther back in the rocks his hiding place turned into another canyon. He started to follow it in, but Buck stopped, tossed his head and snorted in protest.

"What's the matter with you?" Rocklin said. The horse tossed his head again. Rocklin dismounted, took out his hand gun and, leading Buck, edged slowly along the twisting trail — and at the end of it he stumbled onto one of the tragedies that sometimes overtook people on their way West. In another of the numerous desert canyons that wound their hidden, crooked and rocky ways into the mountains, he found an old Conestoga, the bones of an ox and the skeletons of a man and a woman. He had seen such a thing before, once. Probably out of water, one of their oxen dead along the trail, the couple had pulled their other exhausted ox into the canyon, looking for shade along its steep side.

There was a rusty old .45-caliber Colt revolver near the larger skeleton of the man and a piece of his skull was gone. The woman had also been shot in the head — it was better than dying of dehydration — and her bones were in a huddled position on the remaining shreds of a blanket under the wagon. She had probably died when she was asleep, or had been pretending to be.

Looking around, Rocklin could see that someone had previously discovered the scene. There were the empty remains of a strong box, and burnt into its side was a name that Rocklin made out as Rutledge. It had been shot open.

Someone had pried some boards loose from the bed of the wagon, but there had been no hiding place there. The staves of the water barrels hanging from either side of the wagon were dirty gray and sere, shrunken away from the hoops that were dangling uselessly. The bottom was coming out of one of the barrels and there appeared to be something inside. Rocklin found there an almost disintegrated leather bag and one hundred twenty-dollar gold pieces. The gold, he thought, looking around at the ruin of the once fine workmanship of God and man, was in excellent condition.

Rutledge. He would have to find out who they were and try to locate family. The couple had not planned badly, but some misfortune, some miscalculation, who could tell what, had caught up with them on the trail. They had been within a mile of water at the end.

By the time he had worked his way down the western side of the mountains to the valley's wide opening into the hot and dry southern plain — he knew it was hopeless trying to find a sign there anyway because of the cattle trails — and back up, and down the east side and back up, the area was like home to him. And even so, he almost missed what he was looking for.

It was the freak thunderhead that did it. When it started he found a deep cut in a cliff for Buck and a deadfall for himself, spread his slicker over the deadfall, secured it and crawled under. The thunderstorm passed on quickly, leaving freshets here and there where there had been small dry stream beds. But there was a larger stream too, much larger, where none had been before.

He had collected Buck and almost moved on when he stopped to wonder where that large stream had come from. He hadn't remembered a water-worn rock or any kind of declivity above him, and he had long since learned never to ignore the pull of curiosity. Leading Buck, he started up the steep, wooded slope. An hour later he found a cleft in the mountain rock, like a cave. The water was coming from the cleft. There were crags above the hole, and beyond, seemingly only a stone's throw away, a perpendicular rise to the ragged peaks.

He told Buck to wait and started working his way up one of the crags. It took another hour, but at the top he looked down the other side into a small green valley. He could hardly believe his eyes. The stream was pouring into the crag more than a hundred feet below, through a hole hardly big enough for a large man to crawl through. And there, scattered across the grassy valley, were the missing cattle.

They must have brought the cattle, a few at a time, around the southern end of the Sweetwater, where there were signs of ten thousand cows, up a mountain slope from the desert side and into an opening so narrow that no one suspected it was there.

Rocklin studied the far side of the tiny valley through his glasses and thought he could see where the opening from the desert might be. He would find it later. He was satisfied, and besides, he needed supplies. It was time to go into town and get acquainted.

He was less than a four hour ride from the pass where the stage road that he had followed south started to wind down into the valley, but it was past noon and he figured it was another half day's ride to the town. He decided not to hurry; he disliked hurrying, anyway. He found a safe spot, unsaddled Buck, made some coffee, chewed some jerky and rested. Buck shifted for himself.

He was following an old game trail a few hours later when Buck stopped, his head up and ears pointed forward. Many minutes passed while horse and rider waited and listened. Finally Buck settled down and Rocklin dismounted and led his horse higher into the timber, away from the old trail. He hadn't heard what Buck had heard; in fact, he hadn't heard anything, but he worked slowly forward in a gradual circle, just in case.

The sun was vanishing below the peaks to the west when Buck stopped again to listen, his nostrils flaring.

"What is it?" Rocklin said, as much to himself as to the horse. It sounded faintly like a trapped animal thrashing weakly about. Rocklin listened long enough to pinpoint the location and started slowly in that direction, stopping every few yards to listen.

He had moved perhaps a hundred yards in half an hour and had again stopped to listen, when he heard an unmistakable low moan. It came from a clump of juniper just ahead. He heard painful breathing and moved ahead with deliberate speed. He found a boy, half conscious, half delirious, burning with fever and with a gunshot wound in his left shoulder. There were two dead quail tied to a rawhide thong at the boy's waist, but no gun. He had probably dropped it when he was shot.

Rocklin picked the boy up and started toward a small cave that had been cut out of a large sandstone rock about a quarter of a mile back. The boy fought him weakly and Rocklin said, "Easy son. Easy. You're in no condition for a scrap." Buck followed along as though willing to help, but the boy was not heavy in the arms of Rocklin, who was a powerful man under his unprepossessing exterior.

He quickly gathered underbrush and piled it in a semicircle in front of the cave as a screen, collected a pile of wood and built a fire, filled his coffee pot with water from his canteen and started it heating. The boy was half conscious and he struggled a little when Rocklin gently stripped off his denim jacket and shirt. The wound didn't look good, but the bullet had gone through. Rocklin unstrapped his bedroll and made the boy as comfortable as he could and went foraging. He found some skunk cabbage and smart weed, or at least the local equivalent. Using the plants, some of the rough tobacco he occasionally enjoyed in a pipe, and hot water, he made large poultices and secured them front and back with the boy's shirt. There was no protest; the boy was unconscious. The quail were still good. He cut one up to boil it for broth and roasted the other one and ate it.

He changed the poultices five times in twenty hours, and it wasn't until the last time that he began to hope. Meanwhile he had scouted around and found the boy's gun and the tracks of his horse. There were no signs that the horse had been injured and it had probably headed home.

The boy regained brief consciousness several times in those hours, and one time he sat up suddenly and looked around trying to get his bearings.

"Lie still son," Rocklin told him. "You're in bad shape."

"Who are you?"

"I'm the man who'll save your bacon if you do just what I tell you."

"I was shot."

"You sure were. And you have blood poisoning in a bad place. It hasn't gone any farther, but your fever hasn't broken yet. Just lie still and don't talk. I'm going to feed you a little broth from the quail you shot. You're very lucky to have them."

"It wasn't luck; I aimed at them" the boy said, and he lay back and closed his eyes.

Oddly, the matter-of-fact remark heartened Rocklin. For the first time he felt that the boy was going to make it.

The wounds didn't look so bad the last time Rocklin changed the poultices. The boy's temperature was down, and he was fully awake.

"Who are you, sir?"

"Name's Rocklin. What's yours?"

"Jimmy MacCrue. How long have I been here?"

"Here? A day or so. I think you had been lying where I found you for at least a day. You're a tough young man. Will anyone be looking for you?"

"Don't know. I've been out this long before, but . . ."

"But what?"

"Well . . ."

"I need to decide what I should do," Rocklin said. "You can't move for a while. Should I stay with you? Or should I ride into town or to a ranch and tell someone?"

"Oh. Well, can't I . . ."

"No you can't," Rocklin said.

"Well . . . my brother and I have been sticking pretty close to the ranch lately. I guess he'll be wondering."

"And your horse will show up without you. All right. I can't leave you now. I'll wait till tomorrow and maybe go fetch him. We'll see."

While Jimmy was thinking this over he dropped off to sleep. Ten hours later he woke up, with no fever and ravenously hungry. He finished off the rest of the broth and the thoroughly boiled chunks of quail.

"How did you find me, sir?" He asked Rocklin.

"Just luck. Happenstance. How far is it to your ranch?" Rocklin asked, although he knew the answer.

"A couple of hours by trail. An hour if you go straight . . ."

Rocklin eyed him. "Then I'll go straight."

"It's pretty steep. It's pretty dangerous." Jimmy protested.

Rocklin got the message. If he approached the ranch house from the back he might well be shot. "All right," he said, "I'll just ride straight in. How about that?"

"It would be better if I went too."

"No. Even when we do start down I'll rig a travois."

"I won't ride it. I feel fine."

"Yes you will, son. It's only in dime novels

that men get shot and then go galloping around over the country."

"It's only my shoulder," Jimmy protested.

"Yes, and you were very lucky. All kinds of muscles and nerves join up at the shoulder. You could easily have been stove up for life."

"How do you know so much?" Jimmy asked, not being impertinent.

"I'm three times your age, son. Now, will you be all right? You'll stay right where you are and rest?"

"Maybe we could signal," Jimmy said. "If you fired three shots kind of slow, my brother would know."

Rocklin thought this over. "Did you see who shot you?" he asked.

"No."

"He was above you and to your right."

"I didn't see anything. I was just . . . shot."

"Could the man who shot you *think* that you saw him?"

"I don't know." Jimmy searched Rocklin's face. "You think he might come back?"

"I'll ride in. You stay put. Are you sure you feel all right?"

"A little dizzy."

"Oh. Is it bad?"

"No, honest, just a little."

"It's the stuff in the poultice. If it gets too bad take the poultice off."

"What is it?"

63

"Tobacco. Skunk cabbage, smart weed. Pretty strong medicine."

"Did you save my life?"

"Probably. Now remember, lie low and rest. I'll leave a gun. All right? We'll be back before dark."

There was no one at the Bar M. Rocklin scouted around. The house was large, for this country, and well-built of timber and stone, with a wide porch. Inside, there were solid floors of carefully hewn planks, and there were Indian rugs, and lights and shadows from ample windows. There was an upstairs, like a loft, with two bedrooms, and a good kitchen, which was adobe and probably the original ranch house. To Rocklin's surprise, the kitchen had a large wood-burning range and a small indoor pump. It was a remarkably good house that bespoke of intelligence, industry and thrift. Outside there was a vegetable garden and smokehouse, a small bunkhouse, unused now but with room for eight men, a large corral and a barn. Clearly, Alex MacCrue's parents, when they were alive, Alex himself, and Jimmy too, never stopped working except to eat and sleep.

Rocklin rummaged around. He took some coffee, sourdough bread and a stew pot from the kitchen. He found some clean rags for bandages and a large jar of patent medicine ointment with a label that made preposterous and amusing claims. Rocklin smelled it and was further amused to find that it undoubtedly contained some of the same things he had been using to make his poultices. He took it along. He found carrots and onions in the garden and a large, meaty soupbone in the smokehouse.

He considered the pros and cons of leaving a note and decided he had to, despite the risk that some intruder, up to no good, would find it. He kept it as cryptic as possible. "You don't know me. I'm not an enemy. Found Jimmy. He is all right but he's been shot and can't be moved for few more days. Took some supplies. Small sandstone cave. Straight up." He had decided to tack the note inconspicuously on the northwest corner of the barn, and he felt sure that Alex MacCrue would scout his own ranch before he rode in, see the note and read the clue.

He had put Buck in the barn so he could eat some hay and also be out of sight, and he had tacked up the note, stuffed his provisions in a gunny sack and was about to lead Buck into the open when he caught a movement from the corner of his eye.

He drew back into the shadows and studied the north wall of the canyon. He wondered if anyone could have heard the tapping of his gun butt when he put up the note. He wondered if

Alex could be coming cautiously home. Then he stopped wondering, since it did no good, and settled down to watch. He saw the movement again and came alert. It was a man climbing up the side of the canyon at least a mile away. Rocklin got his glasses and watched. The man surely wasn't Alex MacCrue. He was dressed in a rather flashy way and wore two guns, and his movements were furtive. He looked around constantly, obviously to make sure he wasn't being observed; so, just as obviously, he hadn't seen Rocklin or suspected his presence on the ranch.

As Rocklin watched, the man climbed a rock, stood on his toes and pushed what appeared to be a flatish saddle wallet or dispatch case into a crack in the rock. Then he climbed down and rode away.

Rocklin waited a full hour in the barn and then rode out of the canyon. He circled around to the north to start up the mountain and headed along the game trail. The light was going fast when he reached the cave.

Jimmy was sitting up pointing the gun at him when he walked around the screen of brush.

"Good boy," Rocklin said.

"Where's Alex? Where's my brother?"

"He wasn't home. Probably out looking for you. Does he know this place?"

"Course."

66

"Good. He'll be along, then. I left a note."

Jimmy considered this. "Isn't that as bad as shooting off a gun?"

Rocklin smiled. "You'll do," he said. "It wasn't a very clear note and I left it in an unlikely place. I think Alex . . . Alex?" Jimmy nodded. "I think he'll find it and get the message. Meanwhile, how hungry are you?"

"I could eat horseshoes."

"It won't be long. Are you still dizzy?"

"Yes. Some."

"I'll build up the fire a bit and put on some water and then take the poultices off." He unloaded the gunny sack, broke off a piece of the bread and handed it to Jimmy. "This will hold you over."

Jimmy chewed bread while Rocklin fed and stirred up a hot fire and put the pot on. While Rocklin was changing the bandage on his shoulder, Jimmy asked, "Were you in our house?"

"Of course. It's a very good house."

"Is it?" Jimmy looked pleased.

Rocklin looked at him. "You and your brother don't visit around much, I take it."

Jimmy didn't reply directly. "I don't remember anyone ever coming to our house," he said.

Rocklin worked silently for a while, putting on clean bandages with the milder ointment, putting the beef bone in the pot and cutting in some carrots and onions.

"What's a dime novel?" Jimmy asked.

"A dime novel? Well, it's a cheap book about adventures in the Wild West, mostly ridiculous. You mean you haven't read any Wild West tales? Why, some youngsters back East read them so much that something goes wrong in their head and they run away to be cowboys, and mostly land in some kind of trouble, or even get killed."

"Billy the Kid rode through Sweetwater once before Pat Garrett shot him."

"You couldn't have been old enough to remember that."

"Older kids told me."

"Well, now there's a good example. Billy wasn't too bright, really, and probably not too sane. When youngsters like him get their heads full of wild ideas, they're trouble."

"I bet he was fast with a gun."

"He was quick to kill. That's not the same thing. Always take your time in sizing up a man. If a man is quick to injure or kill, it means he's ready and willing. He'd just as soon do it as not. You can get so you can tell who they are. When you see such a man, avoid him. There aren't too many like that, anyway."

"You mean crawfish?" Jimmy asked in surprise.

"No, just avoid him. Men like that have the edge, you see. It's because they like trouble. But if you do have to come up against one,

68

don't hesitate. That's what being fast means. It doesn't mean a lot of crazy antics with a gun.

"I know a federal marshal in Texas who was after a killer, just like Billy the Kid. He walked into a saloon one day and there the man was. The fool jerked out his gun and fanned off six shots while the marshal was pulling his gun, taking aim and shooting him right between the eyes. Marshals don't do it that way in dime novels."

"Are you good with a gun?" Jimmy asked. "Did you ever kill anyone?"

"I guess you'd say that a lot of men who have been in the West for a long time might have had to kill someone, if only an Indian."

"My brother killed an Apache when he was only my age."

"Because he had to."

"Course. I guess so. He won't talk about it."

Rocklin finished making the soup and Jimmy ate like a trencherman.

"Our teacher won't let us read trash," he told Rocklin, following an earlier train of thought.

"What does she let you read?"

"A lot of history, and about men's lives, and poetry. She even makes us memorize."

"She does? Good. Like what?"

" 'So live that when thy summons comes'," Jimmy declaimed. " 'to join the innumerable caravan which moves to that mysterious realm where each shall take his chamber in the silent

69

halls of death . . .' "

"Very good," Rocklin said. "Do you like literature?"

"I think so. I think I like it a lot. What does Thanatopsis mean?"

"Didn't your teacher tell you? What's her name, by the way?"

"Miss Lee. Her first name's Jenny, but we don't call her that. Sure, I guess. I don't remember."

"Hm. Let's see. It means the consideration of death, or something like that. Ask Miss Lee when you get back to school. She'll appreciate it. When you've eaten all you want, you'd better rest, get some sleep. I'd like to take the soup off and put the fire out. Both can probably be smelled five miles away."

"You don't think the bushwhacker is still looking for me, do you?" Jimmy asked.

"I don't know. Maybe not. It probably isn't very likely. He's not around here, anyway. It's likely we would have heard him. And Buck certainly would. But you need to rest now."

"I think my brother's sweet on Miss Lee," Jimmy said.

Rocklin laughed. "Young man, you must learn to tell less than you know. Get some sleep."

Jimmy lay back, feeling tired. But he didn't want to go to sleep, and cast about in his mind for another interesting topic of conversation.

"We have some poems by William Cullen Bryant in a book at home. And some books by Plutarch and Sir Walter Scott and Robert Burns."

"Do you, now. Have you read them all?"

"Sure. Some more than once."

"If you get some rest, I may be able to take you down tomorrow or the next day."

"Really? Tomorrow?"

"I said, or the next day."

The boy lay back. He was sleepy but his thoughts were still active. "There are some boys at school who like to pick fights."

"With you?"

"No. Not so much. I'm one of the biggest boys, and I'm the best wrassler and I'm stronger than any of them."

"Good. Let's keep it that way. Sleep."

"Are you a good fighter? My brother is. I've seen him lick a couple of cowboys who needed it. I bet he could be a champion boxer."

"There are lots of ways of fighting besides with your fists."

"Sure wrassling . . ."

"I mean with your feet . . ."

"With your feet?"

"With your open hand. With your arms and hands as levers, using your body as a fulcrum . . ."

Jimmy was staring at him suspiciously. "Do you tell stories?"

Rocklin laughed. "Of course not. Seen men in Asia who could throw a grown man clear over their heads. Or disable him with one blow of their open hand. There are a lot of strange things in the world, Jimmy. I'm going to sleep whether you are or not."

"How come you were in Asia?"

"I went to sea for ten years, starting when I was twelve. And I've helped dig mines in several Asian countries."

"Is that what you are, a miner?"

"In a way, yes. Goodnight."

Buck snorted and Rocklin was instantly awake. He lay perfectly still and listened. He looked at the stars through the trees. They had hardly changed position. Buck snorted again and Rocklin told him to be quiet. Another minute of listening, and Rocklin heard what Buck had. Someone was coming up the trail. Rocklin was pretty sure he was walking and leading two horses. Rocklin took the sixshooter he had left with Jimmy, worked his way silently toward the trail and took a position behind a big pine. He didn't have long to wait. The man who was approaching wasn't being stealthy. Just as the man passed the big tree, Rocklin stepped behind him and stuck the gun in his back.

"Hold it," he said. The man stood still.

"I found the note," Alex MacCrue said. "How's Jimmy?"

"How did you happen to find a note?"

"I scouted my place before going in. You knew I would or you wouldn't have put it there."

Rocklin lowered his gun. "Your brother was shot in the left shoulder. He had blood poisoning when I found him, but he's going to be all right."

They walked to the cave and Alex knelt to look at Jimmy while Rocklin fed the fire for more light. "It went in the front and came out the back," Rocklin said. "It didn't hit anything vital. He won't be crippled." Alex was examining the bandages. "I got the clean rags from your house." Alex stood up and studied Rocklin.

"How did you happen to find him?" he asked.

"What difference does it make? You're going to have to learn how to tell a friend from an enemy if you're going to survive the trouble you're in."

"How do you know about the trouble? Who are you?"

"I stopped overnight at Old Lady Wells and got to talking with Whiskers. I'm a mining engineer. Been looking over these hills for a company back East. Name's Rocklin."

"I'm Alex MacCrue."

Alex knelt again to look at Jimmy, then stood, thinking, undecided. "He's pretty sound asleep."

"Probably for some hours."

"You sure he's not any worse than he appears?"

"Yes."

"If I hadn't shown up, how were you going to get him home?"

"Travois. In another day to two."

Alex nodded. "I don't want to wake him."

"But somebody ought to be at the ranch," Rocklin said.

Alex stared at him. "Whiskers must have talked a blue streak." Rocklin shrugged. "Somebody could walk in and burn my place if he knew I wasn't there."

"Could be why he was shot." Rocklin said.

Alex stared. "Kill a boy just to get at my ranch?" Rocklin shrugged. "What are you besides a mining engineer?" Alex asked.

Rocklin ignored it. He could read the mental struggle on the other man's face. He didn't want to leave his brother and he didn't want to leave his ranch unguarded.

"I could stay here and bring the boy down in a couple of days, or I could go down and watch the ranch."

Alex looked at him with something like incredulity. "Why?" he asked.

"Why not?"

Alex couldn't believe it. He walked away a few paces and stopped, apparently lost in thought, and then walked back. "I'd like to be here when he wakes up," he said. Rocklin nodded. He packed his saddlebags, picked up his bedroll, except what Jimmy was using, and put them on Buck. When he was ready and had started leading Buck toward the trail, Alex spoke.

"Mr. Rocklin."

Rocklin turned.

"Much obliged."

Chapter 6

Rocklin beat the night marauders to the ranch by less than an hour. It was a clear night with a moon and he had dismounted at the narrow neck of the canyon and studied the trail. The most recent hoof marks in and out were his and one other rider's, obviously Mac-Crue's. Just the same, he had circled the wide canyon and checked the ranch buildings before he had settled behind some high rocks overlooking the in-bound road. It was a perfect spot, a place to hold off a small army. Clearly, MacCrue wasn't taking any chances.

There were five riders and they approached almost casually, making no attempt at stealth. There was no way they could conceal their approach in any case. Rocklin saw them when they topped a rise more than a mile away. He let them get within a hundred yards. He could easily have scattered them at 300 yards, even

400, with his new 15-shot Winchester, but he had decided that MacCrue wouldn't want any unnecessary killing, and at the farther distances anything—a skittish horse, a rider's sudden movement, a change of gait—could cause him to kill someone unintentionally.

When they were close enough, he fired off eight quick shots. He got off four of them before the riders hit the dirt, so unexpected was his attack. Three hats whipped into the air. He parted one man's hair, dazing him, and winged another, a superficial wound in the arm. The other four shots were in the dirt, within inches of the men's faces. There was a short silence in which the crashing sound of the heavy rifle seemed to reverberate. Then, muttered curses and sundry imprecations. Rocklin waited, silent. One man rolled onto one knee, upright, and went for his gun. Rocklin's shot seared the back of his hand. There was a long and colorful denunciation from the gunman, but everyone had gotten the message. One of them shouted, "Who are you? We just want to talk." Silence. Prolonged. Then one man started for his horse. He mounted and headed off down the road. The others were quick to take the cue, and soon they were all out of sight.

Rocklin settled himself and dozed the rest of the night, relying on Buck to signal any approaching trouble.

The next morning he bathed in an elongated

trough near the bunkhouse, rinsed his clothes and let them dry awhile in the sun, and treated himself to bacon and hot oatmeal in the kitchen. Then he toured the ranch again. It was roughly a square mile and unusually green. The day before he had noticed what appeared to be a cultivated strip beyond the garden, and now he examined it more closely. It was the beginning of a small apple orchard. His admiration of the single-minded Alex MacCrue was growing. He examined a motionless windmill. The water in the large, round, corrugated zinc storage basin was clear and sweet. Farther up the canyon toward the eastern cliff, the cattle, hardly more than 150 head, were scattered. It was good stock that would bring a good price, a mixture of the hardy old range cattle, Herefords and Angus.

Rocklin thought he could see MacCrue's plan. In a few more years, with a combination of farming and ranching, the place would be almost self-sufficient, and MacCrue's cattle business would be almost pure profit. Buyers would come to him, take his stock at a discount and assume all the risks of getting them to market. At the rate railroads were being built, Rocklin thought, there might be a branch into the valley before many more years.

He was standing by the windmill, looking around the spread, musing, when he idly turned the valve on a pipe sticking out from a

"T" in the line from the well. It gushed water in a stream ten or twelve feet long. Rocklin, astonished, looked up at the windmill, although he knew it wasn't turning. There was no noise. There was no wind. An artesian well. He suddenly had a clearer understanding of the stakes in the mysterious Sweetwater range war. And that was surely what it was, because in this part of the West water was everything. Two years of drought, no snow pack on the mountains, and Sweetwater would be in for some hard times. It had probably seen them before. Rocklin decided that the young Alex MacCrue was one careful Scotsman.

Rocklin waited until dark to take up his post again and had just settled in when he heard MacCrue coming up the trail. He was leading Jimmy's horse and dragging Jimmy on a travois. Rocklin waited out of sight until they had entered the mouth of the canyon and stopped.

"Any trouble?" MacCrue asked.

"Some. Last night. Five men. I discouraged them and they rode away. There's some venison stew on the stove. How are you doing, Jim?"

"Fine." It was a weak response.

"He looks peaked," Alex said. "I'm afraid he got too tired. The stew will be welcome. You might as well come in with us. It's not likely that they'll hit us two nights in a row."

"No. They don't know what the situation is now. They'll want to think it over. But I'll wait till it gets a little darker. I don't want to be seen taking sides."

Jimmy was all questions when Rocklin arrived at the ranch house. Alex had made a comfortable pallet near the fireplace using two ticks from the bunkhouse that he stuffed with hay—called "Montana feathers" by the cowhands.

"Did you say five? Did you hit any of them? Did they shoot at you?"

"Whoa!" Rocklin laughed. "You're sure a bloodthirsty stripling. A few scratches; that's all. Your brother wants to avoid any killing if he can."

"You make good stew," Alex said. "I'll get you some."

"No thanks. I had some earlier. Coffee will be fine."

"I'll bet they aimed to kill *us!*" Jimmy said.

"Maybe," Rocklin agreed. "But remember, you're a human being with a brain. You have choices."

"Before, you said not to hesitate." Jimmy probed.

"If it comes to that, yes. But remember, first you try to avoid unnecessary trouble. Then you try to forestall it . . ."

"What's forestall mean?"

"Head it off."

"How?"

"There are many ways. The situation itself

81

will usually suggest a way. Something as simple as a friendly 'good morning,' or 'howdy' might do it. It's been known to happen that a man makes a friend of an enemy. The main thing, Jimmy, is to use your head. Don't be pushed into something you'd rather avoid just because of someone else's idea of what you ought to do."

Jimmy took some time to mull this, and Alex returned with cups and a gallon-size coffee pot.

"Actually," Rocklin said, "most men will let you be. But there will be a few, no doubt, who will hate you practically on sight for some reason of their own. There's no point in trying to understand it. And if such a man is a killer . . . well, you can tell, that's all. When you can see what he intends to do, do it first. That's what I mean by not hesitating."

Jimmy was frowning, so serious that Rocklin had to smile. "The truth is," he said, "that most men live their whole lives without ever coming up against such a problem. Even in the Wild West."

It was Alex who asked the question that had been on Jimmy's mind: "Why did you choose to help us?"

Rocklin took a couple of swallows of coffee, and then spoke slowly. "I suppose there was no choice, at first. I couldn't just ride on and let the boy die. After that . . ." Rocklin shrugged.

"Are you actually looking for minerals?"

Rocklin eyed Alex MacCrue. The question, and especially the way it was put, was a direct challenge, or it was the question of a man who had decided that a friendship exists. Alex met the older man's gaze. Rocklin glanced at Jimmy and then back at Alex. The message came across immediately: Little pitchers have big ears.

"Yep," Rocklin said. "And it would hamstring me if anyone suspected I was here for any other reason. It might do worse than hamstring me. I understand there have been bushwhackings."

"Jimmy will say absolutely nothing," Alex said.

"School isn't out yet, is it?" Rocklin asked.

"Forget it. He'll say nothing."

"That right, Jim?" Rocklin asked.

"Yessir. You saved my life."

"Good. You could be saving mine." Rocklin turned to Alex. "I'll be leaving in a day or two. I think I've found the back way out, but is there any way a man can see directly into your place here without being seen himself?"

"No."

"Then I probably haven't been spotted. I've been careful."

"Are you sure you'll be able to make it out the back way?"

"I think so. I've seen it from the top and the

83

bottom. I'll make it."

Rocklin left the ranch just before daybreak, but before he left the box canyon he detoured along the wall to the spot where he had seen the man hide something and found it pretty readily. It was an old Army dispatch case full of money. Rocklin slipped it back into its hiding place.

The back way out was a rough, rocky, switchback trail, but Rocklin led Buck and they made it to the old game trail by seven in the morning. They didn't turn west toward the pass, however. Rocklin had decided he wanted to investigate one more thing and it wasn't far away.

The hole that the water had flowed through from the kitchen valley was plenty big enough for a man to crawl through, but it was a hundred yards long and there were turns. The sand had been tamped down by the water and there was a hard, crusty surface four or five inches thick. It was easy going except for the stretches where no light showed from either end. And at that, Rocklin was lucky. He had gotten far enough toward the valley end of the water tunnel to have some dim daylight coming through when he saw and heard the rattler just in front of him, coiled to strike.

Rocklin froze. He had a healthy respect for

rattlesnakes. He had seen a young cowhand, showing off, grab one by the tail and snap it like a whip, popping its head off, but he had also known men who had lost the use of a hand or a foot because of a bite. He knew a man who had crawled out of his bedroll and put his hand down on the old severed head of a rattler, and the venom had still been potent enough to almost cost the man the use of that hand.

Rocklin edged back slowly and the snake's rattle became more urgent. He knew he wasn't quite within striking distance, and the snake knew it too. They studied each other, the intelligent man and the primitive reptile, the man using his eyes and the snake using its tongue and its sensory pits, which told it that it was confronting a large, warm-blooded creature of some kind. When Rocklin shifted his weight to reach his knife, the snake shifted its aim to the moving arm. Rocklin eased the knife out with almost imperceptible movement but the snake detected the very change in atmosphere and rattled more wildly. It made no move to attack, and, Rocklin decided, probably wouldn't unless it perceived itself to be trapped. Time went by with terrible slowness as Rocklin changed his hold on the knife, getting it in striking position. It crossed his mind that it was a weird face to face battle, with the snake as aware of the stakes, in its way, as the man was. But it was not an even fight. The man had his arm and his remarkable hand. He had a weapon, a large game-skinning knife with an eight-inch blade of the hardest forged steel, very sharp. The snake had its coil-spring body and its fangs and its little bags of deadly venom. But it was a small snake and Rocklin knew it couldn't strike any farther than three-quarters of its length.

Rocklin had a sour taste in his mouth. It was time to get it over with. He feinted with the knife; the snake struck, far short, and had hardly started its recoil when Rocklin's knife took its head off. Rocklin chopped into the crusty sand with his knife, dug a hole and buried the dangerous head.

It was a tighter squeeze on the valley side of the watercourse, and Rocklin scraped the sand away to make it a little easier. The pile of rocks and the tall grass around the hole were undisturbed. The rustlers who used the valley probably didn't even know it was there. It was a bright day and there was the sound of birds in the grass, and Rocklin didn't want to startle them. He paused just a few minutes, studying the terrain through his glasses. He could see one man, high on a rock where he judged the entrance of the valley to be. There was a small line shack in the vicinity. Probably two men, at most, who spelled each other at guard duty.

Rocklin edged back into the cave, pulled as

many rocks around the opening as he could; and started back.

He followed the old game trail, past the cave where he had holed up with Jimmy, past the trail, completely hidden by brush, that led down to the Bar M, and was about to break out into the road to the valley when he heard gunshots, quite a few of them.

"Hell, I'm never going to get to town," he muttered to Buck as he pulled up. He found a vantage point and saw five riders chasing one rider straight up the valley toward him. The men of the posse, if that's what it was, were throwing shots at the lone rider, who was not trying to shoot back but just increasing his distance. Rocklin settled back and took out his glasses. He thought he recognized the man who was trying to escape, and was sure he recognized two or three of the pursuers. One of them was the young man in the fancy get-up who had hidden the money on MacCrue's place. Two others he remembered seeing through his glasses when he had studied the Belsher spread on his reconnaissance of the valley.

They were very noticeable men, huge, at least six-feet-four with shoulders three feet across, and they were identical. Both wore bat-wing chaps, as though they were bronc riders, and the thought crossed Rocklin's mind that they were probably good at their job, since their sheer size would just plain wear a horse down.

But it was the man on the run who interested Rocklin most. He was sure he recognized him as a man of questionable antecedents who called himself Jack Rooney and was a some-time outlaw, bounty hunter and range detective.

Rooney had outdistanced his pursuers. He pulled up just off the stage road and took a good position behind a rock. The five men soon came into sight down the hill but had slowed down considerably. Soon, they stopped to study the trail. It was plain that there were many places where a desperate man could lie in ambush. They listened, heard nothing, and came slowly on, leading their horses. When they were almost ahead of Rooney, he stood up on the rock above them, rifle pointed, and said, "Hold it right there."

One of the men went for his gun and Rooney shot his cartridge belt off. "I said hold it. I just want to talk. Now. Is anyone in charge of you fools?" The men stirred. "You look like cow-hands to me . . . and you, with the fancy guns, make one more move and I'll shoot you right between the eyes." Everyone waited. Time seemed to wait. "Well," Rooney said, "is any-one going to tell me what this is all about?"

The man with the fancy guns said, "I'm the Laredo Kid." He waited for a reaction that didn't come and then blurted, "There's been a stage robbery."

Rocklin could hear the talk clearly. After considering the situation, he thought it might be a good idea to butt in. He mounted Buck and started at a relaxed pace down the trail.

"Is that what you do when there's a robbery? Just pick out some stranger at random and start shooting?" Rooney demanded.

"You were on Double B land," Laredo said.

"I was not. I was on the road. And you people just came at me. When was the stage robbed?"

"Five days ago." Laredo said.

Rooney laughed. "Why you fools, I was nowhere near here five days ago. Does everybody in this valley shoot first and ask questions later? You're damn lucky I didn't kill a couple of you."

"You could have rode out and come back," one of the men said, then they all turned to watch Rocklin come down the trail, all except Rooney and the Laredo Kid, who didn't take their eyes off each other.

Rocklin pulled up and said, "Howdy." No one said anything. "Did I walk into something?" Rocklin asked in his friendly tone.

"Who are you?" Laredo asked.

"Name's Rocklin." He was watching Rooney from the corner of his eyes but Rooney didn't flick so much as an eyelash.

"Ain't I heard about you?" the Kid asked. "You the mining engineer?"

"The same."

"You know this man?" the Kid asked.

"Nope. Seen him off and on. We've been riding the same direction the last four or five days."

The Kid looked almost relieved. "Then he couldn't have robbed a stage coming down this pass four days ago?"

Rocklin saw the picture at once. It was comical. The Kid did not want anyone but Alex MacCrue accused of that robbery, and here were four of his riders running away from him after somebody else. "Not unless he's twins," Rocklin said.

"Heard you were coming a week ago. What kept you?" the Kid asked. Rocklin touched the brim of his hat, edged Buck around the other horses and went on down the trail. Soon he heard the riders coming at a run, pulled aside and let them go by. He continued to loaf along until Rooney caught up with him.

"So you're Rocklin? Heard of you. But my memory's getting short. Didn't you have some other handle that last time we met?"

Rocklin laughed shortly. "Didn't you?"

"More than likely. You actually looking for something to mine?"

"Yep."

"You picked a fine time to ride down this

90

way."

"So it seems."

"If you're just prospecting, how come you're being so careful?" Rocklin looked a question at him. "I found the two bodies you stashed," Rooney said.

Rocklin shrugged. "Didn't want anyone getting wrong ideas."

After a silence, Rooney said, "They were kin of mine. I was supposed to meet them in Sweetwater."

"They sure did want killing," Rocklin said. "Well, there are some in every family. Were they close?"

"Never saw them before. You did me a good turn with that bunch back there, but those men you killed were kin. It'll have to be settled between us before this is over."

"Why?" Rocklin asked.

They rode together until they reached the town, long after dark, but there wasn't a lot of conversation.

Chapter 7

Jenny Lee was pensive; more, she was depressed, which was rare. It was a Saturday morning, overcast and sullen, which was also rare for Sweetwater.

It had been Jenny's habit for some time to treat herself to a small steak and eggs at the Cattlemen's Hotel on Saturdays. It was an extravagance she needed after a week of teaching the children of the valley, who ranged in age from eight to sixteen. It helped her to keep in touch with the wider world and to resist the subtle pressure from the people she served to fall into the category of "schoolmarm." It was not that the community pressure was overt, or even that the community was fully aware of it; it was just that, being a teacher and relatively young—there were many younger teachers than Jenny in the West, even girls in their teens — she was expected to be circumspect.

At the same time, she was a prize for the remote Valley of the Sweetwater, as the inhabitants well knew. She was pretty as well as attractive, which was not necessarily a job qualification, but was widely appreciated in a community where women were scarce and pretty ones even scarcer. She was a good teacher with far above average credentials, being a graduate of a normal school in the East. She was ladylike and modest, although a bit too independent in her behavior for some people's taste. That independence, however, seemed to spring from the tragic circumstances surrounding her arrival in the valley and was understood by most.

Jenny Lee had come West just after graduating from normal school to meet her older sister Ruby and her sister's husband, Tom Rutledge. She was just eighteen at the time and her parents had died a year earlier. She had arrived on the stage from the north with all of her belongings and just enough money to pay for a hotel room for a while if she had to. Her sister and brother-in-law were bringing a wagon west across Texas from Missouri. They never arrived.

Jenny stayed in the hotel two weeks, and waited no longer. She went to work in the kitchen for a few months, and then Mr. Brandt, the owner of the hotel, was inspired to put her to work in the small dining room. His business, almost all men, picked up immediately.

Jenny was hard-working, invariably cheerful, though not in the least flirtatious, and had a free, no-nonsense walk when she was about her business that the men found uncommonly attractive. Several, young and old, thought about proposing, and some did. When the school was started, Jenny was really the obvious, the only, choice the community had, but even then two or three of the men responsible for the school hesitated to hire her because they liked to see her and be served by her in the hotel dining room. Nevertheless, she was hired as the teacher, and Mr. Higgins, the owner of the bank who had just built a more imposing house, offered his smaller one to her at a nominal rent.

Jenny Lee might have been set on her life's course. But she would not and could not give up hope that her sister would come. Over the early years, that hope became almost a peculiarity. Every weekend she would rent a horse at the livery stable and search the nooks and crannies of the Sweetwater area. She would inquire of any stranger who came to town, and in fact, during the first months of her search, she had talked to a trail boss who had come across Tom and Ruby Rutledge just outside the tiny town of Big Springs, about 150 miles east in Texas, and had found them in good shape and good spirits.

At times, Jenny would take food and a bedroll and wander far off, camping overnight. It was foolhardy and it worried the people of Sweetwater. The ranchers made it clear that she was welcome to spend the night any time, but she rarely did. So the working hands, the men in the line shacks, those moving bunches of cattle from one part of the range to another for better grass, kept an unobtrusive eye on her. As far as the men of the valley were concerned, she was absolutely safe. Few would even think of bothering her, and the few who would think of it wouldn't dare. But there were roving Indians, Apaches. Even so, the community's worry was overblown. The Indians were fully aware of the strange female who wandered about and thought her a bit mad, and therefore avoided her.

But as years passed and as Jenny became more engrossed with her teaching duties and her students—she was a strict and loving teacher and her students would do anything to please her—she searched less often.

The people of the valley became less concerned for her, more accustomed to her, and resigned to the possibility that she would never marry. She was a schoomarm, and in a community like Sweetwater the only females who were allowed to remain single were fallen women and schoolmarms.

Jenny Lee was well aware of her increasingly immutable status in the eyes of the town, and she didn't like it. First, she was not going to marry anyone she didn't love and want. She could have done that at any time, and had even turned down an offer to become the mistress of the grandest house on the biggest spread in the valley—and that was one secret that only the two participants would ever know about. She was also well aware of the large body of opinion in the community that a woman who refused to marry just because she wasn't "in love" was being selfish and whimsical.

And she wondered about Alex MacCrue. Jenny had a vivid memory of the first time she had seen him. She had been groping her way out of oblivion into flashes of brilliant red and white sunlight, and he had been squatting beside her pouring the cool contents of a full canteen over her head and face and neck.

It had been a long weekend because of a short school week and Jenny had ridden farther south into the lower plain beyond the valley than she had thought, wandering down hidden arroyos and crisscrossing the precipitous edges of the mountains on the desert side looking for sandy canyons, obscure trails and forbidding rock formations—anything unexpected in the wild terrain that might hide the story of her sister's fate.

She was tired and hot and thirsty when she found to her dismay that her canteen was almost empty. She turned back immediately, wondering how far she had come from the spot at the lower end of the valley where Sweetwater Creek twisted down a rocky wash and disappeared into the earth. She thought it couldn't be more than a few miles.

In fact it was ten miles, the sun was directly overhead, and the occasional breeze from the north blowing across her perspiration-damp shirt made her feel marvelously cool and free. She did not notice that no living thing stirred on the desert floor, and she did not dream that her feet would blister through her boots if she dismounted and walked any distance at all to give her horse a rest.

She was beginning to weave in the saddle when she drank the last of her water and saw the beginning of the grass in the lower valley. It was deceptively close; just a mile or so, she thought. But it was closer to three. She didn't make it. She saw strange red flashes and started to fall.

Alex MacCrue was pushing about twenty head of cattle north toward the creek. He had been out six days and was glad to be on his way home; but he was also edgy. It was apparently true that cattle were wandering off never to be seen again. None of his, it seemed, but other brands. The talk had been spreading for two or three months, and now he believed it. At first he had not, because he knew it was no easy matter for anyone to casually run off a few head of cattle from the Sweetwater and find a ready market. The desert was too open; the water holes were too few and far between. Why would anyone risk it? And where could they take them?

He had decided to ride out and see for himself. He knew the valley well, and all the brands, and how many cattle each rancher ran. There were few secrets among the cattle-men.

But there it was: Cattle were indeed missing—but none of his. He decided to round up the few he had on the open south range and take them back to his canyon.

He hadn't had to cover too much of the hundred square miles before he had brought them together, but he had covered enough of it to have crossed Jenny Lee's trail several times since the beginning of the weekend. Apparently she had gone out into the desert and not come back. It was worrisome.

He had heard her story, of course—Jimmy happily kept him up to date about the goings-on in town—and he had seen her a time or two, once close enough for him to see the shine on her shoulder-length chestnut hair. And he had wondered idly if she was a little touched, as the Indians who wandered off of the Apache reservation to the west thought she was. At least on the subject of her sister. But Jimmy liked her, and thought she knew everything.

The cattle were on their way to the creek, now, smelling water, and for the twentieth time MacCrue stopped, turned his horse and studied the terrain sloping down to the south. There was a horse and rider in the distance, four miles at least, and the horse was either moving very slowly or had stopped. Too far away to tell. But the rider seemed to be dismounting. Or, Alex suddenly thought, falling.

Alex headed south, thinking that the cattle would stay around the water for awhile; and even if they didn't, it would take only a day to round them up again.

Jenny was lying on the ground, her face exposed to the sky, and Alex's first thought was that she had been lucky to have fallen on the shady side of her horse. If she had not, her face would have been badly burned and possibly her eyes permanently damaged. Her skin was dry and hot. Alex soaked his bandanna with water from his canteen and put it over her eyes; then he poured some of the water over her head and face. She stirred and then started up.

"Be still," he said.

It was an unnecessary caution. Jenny's head spun and she sank back on his arm. He put his canteen to her lips and she drank, but she felt that she was going to retch. She turned her head away and swallowed spasmodically.

"You need salt," he said. "Just a minute." He got up, dug into his saddle bags and came back with salt, which he put in her hand. "Lick it and then take a couple of

101

swallows of water. Can you do that?"

"I can't —"

"Do it. It will settle your stomach."

She did as he said and then settled back dizzily on his arm. He wiped her face gently with the wet bandanna, poured the rest of the water on it, spread it over her head and put her hat on.

"No more water?" she whispered.

"We'll get some more. The main thing now is to get you cooled down, and the sooner the better. I'm going to take you to the creek."

"I can't."

"You can. Now. I have to get you off this ground."

"Snakes," she muttered vaguely.

"No snakes," he said. "A snake wouldn't be foolish enough to be out in this. You're burning up."

"You're out in it," Jenny mumbled, and Alex MacCrue felt a strange tender exasperation.

He lifted her easily and mounted, set her across his legs to let her head rest on his shoulder, and headed for the creek in a hurry. Her skin was still very hot when they reached the water and she was not fully conscious. The water was shaded and cool under the cottonwoods, and he laid her in it flat on her back, his hand pillowing her head so that her face and ears were just above the surface. She protested and squirmed a bit but he was firm, and soon with a deep sigh she lay back and rested. He bathed her face with his bandanna and watched the pulse in her throat gradually slow.

It was half an hour before she was strong enough to protest that she was all right.

"Are you planning to drown me," she asked in a small voice.

He smiled—rare for him—and helped her sit up in the creek. He got his bedroll, spread it on the ground and picked her up and laid her on it. Then he filled his and her canteens and helped her drink. She was watching his face and he noticed that her eyes were dark brown, almost the color of her hair.

"Thank you, Mister—"

"MacCrue." He stood up abruptly and turned to see to his horse, which was almost exhausted.

"Oh." She paused, considering her impression that her thoughts had somehow slowed down. "Then you're Jimmy's brother." Alex nodded and went on unsaddling his horse. "I've heard about you."

He didn't say anything and she was not surprised. It wouldn't occur to him, she

103

thought, to ask what she had heard. She watched him wipe his horse down with his wet bandanna and wondered about her own mount.

"My horse—"

"It'll be along. The reins weren't trailed. It'll find the water." He dug some jerky out of his saddlebags and offered her a piece. She was collecting wet strands of her hair, wringing them out and combing them back with her fingers.

"No thank you," she said. "I don't really like it much."

"It's salty; it'll do you good."

She took it meekly and sat chewing it, watching him as he finished with his horse. He was aware of her eyes on him and the awareness irritated him. It was as though he could still feel the movement of her strong back under his arm and he wondered about it, whether it was improper, and whether it showed on his face. She was studying his scowl, puzzled, when he sat against a tree, pulled his hat over his face, stretched out his legs and folded his arms across his chest. She felt a contrary urge to keep his attention.

"I suppose you saved my life," she said.

"Rest," he said from under his hat.

"How can I rest in sopping wet clothes?"

"They'll help keep you cool. And they'll dry out soon enough. Rest."

She lay back, pillowed her head on her arm, and was out so quickly that she was not even aware that she was dozing off.

She awoke slowly, sat up lazily and looked around. Alex MacCrue was checking the saddle on her horse and stowing some hardtack and salt pork in her saddlebags. The shadows were longer but the sun was still bright and hot, and her clothes, except where she had been lying on them, were dry.

When Alex saw her watching he said, "I have to go. You'll be all right here?"

She almost asked him why he couldn't stay. "Of course," she said.

"Rest overnight. I laid a fire for you."

When he had mounted she said, "Mr. Mac-Crue. Thank you." And he nodded, touched his hat and rode away.

She had seen him on rare occasions since then, when he had come into town for such supplies as coffee and flour and salt, but he had seemed, as always, wild and wary and uncommunicative. (Jimmy, an intelligent and personable boy, had been developing the same mannerisms when Jenny took him in hand.)

Yet she felt she knew Alex MacCrue a little. She knew that he had lost his parents, and she knew of his lonely fight to hold on to his ranch; the whole valley knew of it and granted him a sometimes grudging respect. Some thought he was a fool; others were almost in awe of him. But Jenny thought she knew what he was going through. They were, after all, contemporaries, the same age in fact.

Two or three times after he had saved her from the desert, however, she had encountered him on her rides, and his offers to ride with her a ways had seemed so curt that she had rejected them.

And then when he had seen her with the Laredo Kid and had, in effect, told her to behave (incredible!) she had walked home in something like a rage, breathless, her heart pounding with indignation. And whenever she recalled the incident, as she did several times, her heart pounded with the same indignation.

It was pounding now, on this oppressive Saturday morning. But at least the indignation was better than depression, and better too than the sense of disorientation that had come upon her several times in the past month or so when she felt that her familiar surroundings were unfamiliar, that she was a stranger from somewhere else.

She was standing in her small sitting room, uncharacteristically undecided, and she could see the town through the lace curtain on the small dormer window. She could see Mr. Rocklin, the pleasant and educated man who had been staying at the hotel for about two weeks, see him hail Alex MacCrue as though he knew him. She was surprised; Mr. Rocklin seemed to be trying to persuade Alex to go with him to the hotel dining room. She was astonished; Alex was going. Jenny doubted that Alex MacCrue had ordered anything in a restaurant in his entire life. She saw the two men encounter Mr. Higgins and thought she saw—though it seemed unlikely—Mr. Rocklin introduce Alex MacCrue to the town banker.

Jenny Lee took her shawl, a lovely mantilla given to her by one of the ranchers' wives, and went to have breakfast.

The three men got to their feet when Jenny entered the dining room. Rocklin said, "Good morning, Miss Lee." Higgins nodded and said, "Miss Lee." Alex, taking a slow, deep, and he hoped, inconspicuous breath in an effort to control the rush of blood to his head, said, "Morning."

"Are you having breakfast?" Rocklin asked, and when Jenny nodded, said, "We would be mighty pleased if you'd join us."

"Yes, do," Higgins said, and pulled out a chair.

"If you promise not to let me interrupt your conversation," Jenny said. The men smiled indulgently. They had been talking about ranching.

"They have some very tasty bacon," Rocklin said, "supplied, I'm told, by one of the farmers near town."

"Really? It sounds wonderful."

The waitress was a girl from one of the homesteading families and one of Jenny's students. She was quite pretty in her calico dress and starched white apron. Brandt, the owner of the hotel, had recently taken his family to Kansas City on the Sante Fe, traveling to Las Cruces to catch it, and had been impressed with the neat and well-trained serving girls at the Harvey restaurants along the route.

"Crisp?" Rocklin asked.

"Moderately," Jenny told the girl.

"Miss Lee would also like two eggs, fried in butter with the yolks unbroken, two rolls and coffee," Rocklin said.

The girl, who already knew how Jenny liked her eggs, said, "Yes sir."

"You're very observant, Mr. Rocklin," Jenny said.

MacCrue watched all this with his concentrating scowl.

"Your breakfasts are almost ready," the girl told the men. "Shall I wait or bring them now?"

"Oh, please gentlemen," Jenny said, "eat while it's hot, by all means."

"I can wait," MacCrue snapped. The other men said, "Of course."

"I can keep them warm," the girl offered. "It won't take long."

"Then just coffee for now, Maudie." Jenny said. The girl looked pleased with her contribution, and said, "Yes ma'am."

"Alex was telling us his ideas on the future of the cattle ranch," Rocklin said. Higgins, who had a gentle smile, said, "Yes, and very interesting too."

Jenny looked inquiringly at Alex.

Alex felt himself perspiring. He was on the verge of being angry at the other two men, wondering if they had deliberately put him on the spot. He stared at them but they were simply swallowing coffee. The girl brought Jenny a cup, and Alex took a drink of his. Then, with an effort, he met Jenny's gaze.

"I was just saying that this valley is farming

land."

"Really?" Jenny said. "Isn't that an unusual view, for a cattleman?"

"No. I mean, yes. What I meant was that areas like this one . . ." He seemed to be trying to find the right words

"The valley?" Jenny asked.

"Yes. Good farming land, like in the valley, is going to be too valuable for just raising beef."

"I see."

"I want to be ready. With a ranch that will give me everything I need."

"Then you aren't one who would drive off the homesteaders?" Jenny asked.

"What good would it do?" Alex demanded.

Higgins cleared his throat. "Mr. MacCrue was making the point earlier that the railroads are going to lay almost a hundred thousand miles of track in the United States this year alone."

"Yes," Alex said. "And Mr. Rocklin . . . he lives in New York . . . said almost four million people, immigrants, have come through there from Europe in the past ten years alone, and a lot of them will be looking for land."

"I see." Jenny said. "So you think it's inevitable . . ."

110

"That's the way I see it."

"Very interesting. And will the ranchers fight to keep them out?" Jenny asked.

The men didn't say anything. It was extremely touchy subject. Alex looked as if he was sorry he had brought it up. They drank coffee until Maudie brought their food, and then some appreciative remarks were passed about the bacon. It was Jenny who revived the subject because she knew Alex was interested in it and had thoughts about it.

"What do you think, Mr. Rocklin? I have the impression you've seen a great deal of the West."

"I haven't really been—" Rocklin demurred.

"Oh, come on, Rocklin," Higgins said, "answer the lady's question."

"I'm interested, you know," Jenny said. "I have students, and they have a future."

"Well, actually," Rocklin said, "I think the change might come fairly easily here. It's pretty far out of the way, after all. Southern Pacific's transcontinental line is not too far south, but I think any branch line will be a long time coming because there is no market here that is big enough. So by the time the Westward movement reaches here, the pattern will already have been established in the rest of the nation. There will be, as Alex says, a

111

kind of inevitability to it. And there is land to the south, hundreds of thousands of acres, that is good for nothing but grazing."

"You sound as though you know something about ranching," Jenny said.

"I owned a ranch once," Rocklin said. "I sold it."

"Why?" Alex asked.

"I suppose because I thought it had reached the limit of its value," Rocklin said.

"Oh." Alex seemed taken aback.

Higgins said, "I don't know that it's too good a trend, but speculating in ranch property has become quite popular in certain circles in the East."

"How do you know?" Alex asked.

Higgins smiled his gentle smile. "My son is a New York stockbroker, and my daughter is the wife of a New York lawyer. In fact, Mr. MacCrue, if you sold your place to an Eastern syndicate right now, free and clear as it is, you would be a fairly rich man."

"Sell my ranch?" MacCrue was incredulous, as well as immediately suspicious.

"No, no, no. I wasn't suggesting that at all," Higgins said. "I was merely commenting about the market."

"I think it would be hard to find another valley quite so beautiful," Jenny said.

112

Alex looked at her. "It's a hard life out here for a woman," he said. There was a pause as everyone adjusted to this apparent change of subject.

"Not necessarily," Jenny said. "Suppose she loved it? And had someone to cherish?"

"And was also cherished," Rocklin said.

Jenny glanced mischievously at Rocklin. "Of course. Are you married, Mr. Rocklin?"

"Yes, dear child. I'm afraid you're too late."

Jenny laughed. Higgins smiled. Alex's head was buzzing with what he had said, and with the easy humor with which it was handled by the relative strangers at the table.

"I, on the other hand, am a rich banker," Higgins said. His wife had died two years ago, and for a full year, in his deep grief, he had turned to books and had not spoken to anyone except on business.

"Oh, but bankers are so notoriously cold-hearted," Jenny teased.

"Vile calumny!"

"And I, on the other hand," Jenny said, "have a warm heart, some fine napery and silver from my dear mother, a spinet and an indomitable will."

"I'm not sure I like that last part," Alex said, much to his own astonishment. Jenny and Rocklin laughed; Higgins smiled, and Alex tried to control a blush of pleasure.

"It's essential," Jenny said. "Otherwise the man could become a tyrant and the woman a namby-pamby."

"And suppose it turns out the other way around?" Alex asked. Jenny smiled at him with her raised eyebrow trick.

"The operative word, I think, is 'cherish,' " Rocklin said. "Wouldn't you say so, Mr. Higgins?"

"I would. I would indeed." Everyone was silent for a moment, and Maudie brought some more coffee.

After the four of them had finished breakfast, and just as they were leaving the dining room, the Laredo Kid entered. He swept his hat off and gave his mock bow and synthetic smile. "Good morning, Jenny," he said. She nodded pleasantly.

No one missed, nor was anyone fooled by, the crude familiarity. Nor had anyone missed the quick glance of pure hate the Kid had shot at Alex. "I see you still won't wear a gun," he said to Alex with a broad grin. Everyone ignored him.

"I want to walk home with you," Alex said to Jenny, who nodded and said, "I want you to."

Only Maudie took any notice of the Kid, and the look on his face frightened her. She thought for a second that he was going to pull his gun and kill all of them right there.

Rocklin and Higgins watched Alex and Jenny as they went down the sidewalk. "That will be a most interesting union," Higgins said, and Rocklin replied, "I couldn't agree more."

"There were unfortunate circumstances surrounding her coming to the valley," Higgins said, "and she handled them like a thoroughbred."

"Oh?" Rocklin asked.

"I admire the way you handled that," Jenny said. But Alex was on a thought track of his own.

"I've never done anything like that before," he said.

Jenny laughed lightly. "Do you mean eat breakfast?"

"It was . . . well, I mean, after awhile it was exciting."

"Warm human contact," Jenny said. "It comes from liking people."

115

"Yes. Well . . ."

Moments later, when they were nearing Jenny's gate, Alex said, "It doesn't really have to be a hard life."

"Of course not," Jenny said. "Work doesn't make a hard life. Imagine a life with no work! But I've seen some of the women of the valley. The worst thing, I think, is a joyless marriage."

Alex considered this, scowling. "I have a lot to learn," he said.

"You will," Jenny assured him. "You've had a hard time."

"I don't have any chickens yet. Some things I just haven't had time for, but I have a vegetable garden and I've started an apple orchard . . ."

"It sounds wonderful," Jenny said.

"I suppose I could buy some chickens, a rooster and some laying hens from one of the sodbust — one of the farmers."

"I've ridden by your canyon several times," Jenny said, "but I've never actually seen your house."

"Oh. Yes. Well, I wish . . . I mean it's a very bad time in the valley right now . . ."

"I've heard talk," Jenny said. "Are you in trouble?"

"I believe I am."

116

"I see," she said, although she didn't.

They were on the porch, and behind them they heard the gate open. It was Rocklin.

"Oh. Mr. Rocklin," Jenny said. Alex looked surprised, and he was frowning.

"I beg your pardon," Rocklin said, "but I have just learned, Miss Lee, that some time ago you were searching for a couple named Rutledge."

Jenny caught her breath. "Yes. Yes I was. My brother-in-law and my younger sister, Ruby. Oh, please, Mr. Rocklin, do you know something?"

Rocklin looked grave. He wished he had waited for a better time, although he didn't know what good that would have done.

"Well, man," Alex demanded.

Rocklin looked at Jenny and held her eye.

"They're dead?" she asked.

"Not twenty miles from here. I found them and their wagon just about three weeks ago."

"I looked and looked," Jenny said.

"You probably passed within a quarter of a mile of them several times," Rocklin said.

"Don't you want to sit down?" Alex asked Jenny.

"Yes. Please, won't you come in."

"How?" Jenny asked. She was on a small couch and Alex had sat beside her and, apparently unnoticed by either of them, had taken her hand.

Rocklin hesitated. He hadn't been prepared for this. "They ran out of water." Jenny closed her eyes and bowed her head. "There was some money," Rocklin said. "A hundred twenty-dollar gold pieces. Two thousand dollars."

"Can't they be buried here?" Jenny asked. "I want them to be buried properly. Maybe I can order some stones in Jackson."

"I'll take care of it," Alex said.

Chapter 8

Mary Tillman
17 Washington Square Place
New York City, New York

My Dearest Wife,
I take pen in hand to assure you of my continued good health and to tell you that I will be starting home within the next month.

There doesn't appear to be any great mystery here, but it is a tangle that will take a little more time to work out.

You would like this valley. It would be a marvelous place to have a winter home. I may buy a small piece of land to that end. The railroads, in time, will make the area much easier to reach, and the land will surely retain its value.

I am sending a report to Consolidated Mining that may be both good and bad. There is potash here, but the source is still pretty far removed from any transportation. Also, there is oil. There is no doubt about it. I found it in a forsaken place in the desert called Black Basin, because it actually is black. The "black" smells and tastes like petroleum. The basin is about ten miles in diameter, and the black seep is almost in the center of it. Neither man nor beast venture into it, and some of the cowpokes around here think it is a mire. It isn't, but I have heard tell of one man who saw a calf sink into it out of sight. I think that is typical of some of the Western lore that gets into print back East.

Of course I must urge Consolidated to buy it, but before I left, old man Wellington told me the firm wasn't interested in oil at this time. He said the coming of electric lights would undercut the kerosene market! And just a few weeks ago, a Santa Fe divisional superintendent told me that the railroad was running a couple of its engines on oil on an experimental basis! If Consolidated rejects my recommendation, I will surely buy Black Basin myself. I have made discreet inquiries and can probably get it for as little as 50 cents an acre.

I will close now. I must compose a long and rather complicated wire to Bannister in Chicago. I'll have to ride into Jackson tomorrow to send it off, and Jackson is fifty miles away.

You are in my thoughts always. Give my love to Louise and little Bill.

I remain,

Your loving husband,

William R. Tillman

Chapter 9

Rocklin walked out of the telegraph office in Jackson straight into Ed Belsher. He stopped and nodded a greeting, grateful to foresight and luck that he had decided to put the message to Bannister in code and address it to Bannister & Co. at a post office box in Chicago. He was wondering if his surprise and relief showed on his face when he noticed that Belsher himself, who was with another man, appeared for the briefest of moments nonplussed.

When Belsher greeted Rocklin in a friendly way and introduced the man he was with as a Jackson lawyer named Harry Leek, Rocklin made a mental connection to a rumor he had picked up earlier in Sweetwater that someone had been trying to buy out the storekeeper,

Josh Cantwell. According to the story, Cantwell had received several offers for his place from some Jackson lawyer who had declined to name his client. And Cantwell was in town. Rocklin had seen him going into the Jackson freight office earlier that morning.

Rocklin acknowledged the introduction with a "how do" and Leek responded with an expansive "Pleasure. Pleasure" that belied the wary look in his eyes. Rocklin was about to make some casual excuse for moving on when Leek slapped him on the back and said, "Any friend of Belsher is a friend of mine. Say, we were just going over to the hotel for breakfast. Why don't you join us."

Rocklin, who had chatted only briefly with Belsher a couple of times in Sweetwater and had been invited to stay overnight at his ranch if his business ever took him out that way, was about to beg off. But Leek, with a gleaming smile, said, "Come on. Come on. Maybe you can tell us a little bit about the mining business."

Rocklin saw that he was about to be pumped and decided to seize the chance to muddy the water a little and at the same time sharpen his image as a mining engineer, since his story had apparently gotten around in a most satisfactory way.

Leek hardly waited for the coffee to be poured before saying, "Well, Mr. Rocklin, nobody ever accused me of being nosy, but have you come across anything interesting?" Then he laughed heartily at himself for breaking all the rules by being so direct.

Belsher joined the laugh and told Rocklin, "The trouble with Harry is that he'll smell out any chance in a hundred miles to make money."

Rocklin chuckled, joining in the spirit of things, and said, "I'm afraid it's not a glory hole. Sorry, Harry, but it's the kind of thing that will take lots of men and lots of planning and lots of heavy equipment, with a relatively small ROI."

"Oh?" Leek said.

"Return on investment."

"Ah. I see. Yes of course. Uh, what is it?"

Ed Belsher sent a sharp glance at the inquisitive Leek, but Rocklin remained friendly and willing to oblige.

"There are two or three possibilities in roughly the same area. It will probably depend on which substance is most easily extractable from the ore. Of course that hasn't been decided yet. In fact nothing's really been decided. It's all still in the exploratory stage.

125

That's why a number of reports are necessary. The one I sent this morning is my second, and there will probably have to be three or four more." Leek, apparently no fool, was frowning, but he managed to laugh in a self-deprecatory way.

"Where is it?" Belsher asked.

Rocklin managed to look embarrassed — but still friendly. "Well . . . now, that subject is a little touchy." Belsher and Leek looked considerably less friendly. "Let me explain," Rocklin went on. "I mentioned that an operation like this takes a lot of planning. For example, where will we sink the main shaft? Or will it be an open pit operation? Where will we buy supplies we will need on a day-to-day basis — not the big stuff, mind you, but things like lumber and nails and picks and shovels? Will there be a local outlet, or will we have to establish one?

"Will we grade a road, and if so, where? Will the railroad decide there will be enough business — with the ore, and possibly the Sweetwater Valley cattle — to lay a branch line? And if so, which railroad? Santa Fe from El Paso or Southern Pacific from the line they're building into Texas? Will Sweetwater be near enough for the workmen? Or will the company have to build a town of its

126

own."

The two men were listening intently and nodding slowly.

"You see the difficulty?" Rocklin asked. "There will be a lot of economic activity. A lot of land being bought and sold, for example." He paused to stare innocently at his breakfast companions. They had swallowed everything whole—and wanted more.

"I'll tell you a little story. Actually, you might have heard something about it. It was in northeast Oklahoma, not in Indian Territory but up in the tri-state area. A big eastern company decided to open up a completely new field for lead and zinc mining . . ."

"The one you work for?" Leek asked.

"I don't work for a company," Rocklin told him. "I have my own consulting firm."

"Ah. Hmm."

"Things were in the planning stage—that's all, mind you—the planning stage—when the word got out. I tell you, the company was spending half its time trying to plug . . . uh, leaks, Mr. Leek. But word got out."

"You'd think," Belsher said, "that a telegraph office would be a river of a leak." The lawyer turned an incredulous and disgusted eye on the rancher, then quickly looked back at Rocklin.

127

"Oh, all reports are in code," Rocklin said. "Oh, yes. It's standard practice. But the word leaked in Oklahoma just the same. And do you know what happened? Several local businessmen, and a doctor and a couple of lawyers, got together and pooled their money and bought up all the land in sight." Rocklin paused.

"And?" Belsher demanded.

"The company decided against the operation." Both men expelled breath, sat back and glared at Rocklin.

"You see how innocent people — well, more or less innocent — can get hurt?" Rocklin asked. "And do you know what those men did? They filed suit against the company." He looked at Harry Leek.

"Of course," Leek said. "I remember the incident now."

Rocklin was nodding like a cautionary schoolteacher. There had been no such incident.

"They didn't have a prayer," the lawyer said.

"Certainly not. The court threw it out," Rocklin said. "But you see my point."

"Absolutely, absolutely," Leek said. "But of course *you* know what's going to happen."

"Not necessarily. Only the top officers of

128

the company know that for sure. Although it's true that I might guess which way the wind's blowing. After all, they're *my* reports."

The breakfast was over, but Leek was impelled to take one more shot. "Well, Mr. Rocklin," he said, "I told you that any friend of Ed Belsher's is a friend of mine, and I meant it. Now, in the course of all its complicated planning, if your mining company ever feels the need of a legal representative, locally, that is . . . uh, what's the company, by the way? Is its stock traded?"

"I'm afraid not," Rocklin said. "It's a family enterprise. They've never gone public."

Rocklin was needled by a sense of urgency as he headed up toward Goodnight Pass, the higher and more treacherous of the two mountain passes between Jackson and Sweetwater. He figured it would take all of two weeks for the information he had requested of Bannister to reach the stage stop at Old Lady Wells. Bannister, after getting Rocklin's lengthy telegram, would have to wire a man in Santa Fe. That wouldn't take long, but Rocklin knew he had to allow at least a week for the agent in Santa Fe to find and copy the documents he wanted. Then there was the stage trip from Santa Fe to Old Lady Wells. But that should work all right; the schedule fit in; Rocklin had checked it.

It was nothing new, this roundabout way of working; Rocklin was accustomed to it, and he was not an impatient man. He knew that in his business impatience could be fatal. So there was little to do but wait, keep an eye on the situation and try to forestall any blowup. All he needed were eyes in the back of his head and a lot of luck.

Meanwhile — Yes, meanwhile, there was that feeling of urgency. Rocklin decided he had better spend some time putting the whole situation — all the facts he knew as well as his surmises — into a report to Bannister. He did not add the thought "just in case"; that was not the way his mind worked. He would take the report to Old Lady Wells when he went to pick up the material from Santa Fe and trust Whiskers to put it on the stage when it stopped there on its way back to the territorial capital.

And there was something else, a new element. It was not anything that would affect his job in Sweetwater Valley, but it was something that Bannister would want to know about.

It had been stirring in the back of his mind

since he left Jackson. At one point he had pulled Buck gently to a stop and had actually dismounted and walked over to gaze down into Goodnight Ravine, a thousand-foot chasm that dropped off the north side of the crude road. It was a wild and dangerous stretch of country where sudden cloudbursts and numerous rock slides had tumbled more than one wagon and more than one hapless rider into oblivion.

Colorado . . . about five years ago . . . there was a lawyer . . . a crooked lawyer and an ostensible cattleman. The association had been involved in the case; maybe it still was. Little was known about the details; they were hushed up. Rocklin had heard things through some of his contacts, most of them shady characters.

An eastern consortium, backed by some big money and big names, had bought a remote Colorado ranch of more than two-hundred thousand acres with the expectation of doubling its money in two or three years. It was the height of the beef-cattle fever, and the Colorado contacts had apparently had little trouble selling what did not in fact exist. There had been a ranch, a small one with a few buildings and a few cows, but beyond that was useless paper — numerous worthless

131

options, dozens of fraudulent homestead claims under phony names, forged water rights.

And who were the con men? The shyster had called himself Lincoln (Rocklin grunted with sour amusement), Henry Lincoln. And the rancher? Rocklin seemed to remember some odd literary connection . . . What was it?

He climbed on Buck and continued up toward the pass.

Harry Leek and Ed Belsher . . . Something odd had happened in Jackson. Yes. Josh Cantwell had been walking down the main street and was about to encounter Leek and Belsher. Belsher had nodded casually to Leek, as though to a relative stranger, and had turned abruptly into the saloon. Leek had approached Cantwell with an outstretched hand and had been curtly brushed off. With a sidestep and an impatient gesture of dis-'missal, Cantwell had walked on down the street. Rocklin had seen it happen as he was leaving the lobby of his hotel.

And another thing: Rocklin had met Cantwell in front of the general store just as Cantwell was mounting to ride out of town, and had nodded and said hello in a friendly way—and Cantwell had merely glared at him and turned away. Rocklin had watched him thoughtfully as he headed east on the pass road, until his view was blocked by another rider going the same way.

Beecher. That was the name. Elwood Beecher. Ed Belsher. Bannister certainly would want to know about it. Rocklin decided to include his thoughts on the lawyer and the rancher in his comprehensive report.

Buck suddenly arched his neck, and his ears shot forward. Rocklin thought, not for the first time, that Goodnight Pass would be a perfect place for a dry-gulching. The ravine was right there, ready to swallow up man, horse, and anything else that anyone wanted to get rid of. Were the bones of Joe Ferrigan down there? Useless to speculate.

Rocklin dismounted and walked as close as he could get to the south side of the road, away from the ravine. It was the best he could do; there was nowhere to go because a steep and rocky incline walled in that side of the road. He took his gun out and moved slowly ahead toward a point where the road disappeared around a jutting perpendicular rock. He had just seen a way to scale the rock so he could look down on the other side when Josh Cantwell stepped into view. He was cradling a Winchester in his right arm, but he wasn't pointing it. Rocklin put his .38 back in the shoulder holster and said, "Hello again, Mr. Cantwell."

"I want to talk to you," Cantwell said.

"Go ahead."

The calm and affable reply brought Cantwell up short. He studied Rocklin's face and looked him up and down. His voice was slightly less combative when he spoke again.

"A few nights ago, someone set fire to my storeroom out back. I had some five-gallon cans of coal oil back there, and some other supplies that could have gone up like dynamite. It was just lucky that I went out there for something when I did. The whole town might have gone."

Rocklin, who knew the value of listening, waited.

"There have been other things," Cantwell said. "Things missing. A rock slide up here at the pass when there hadn't been any rain for a month, and when a freight wagon with my goods happened to be going over."

"It looks like mighty unstable terrain," Rocklin said, glancing around. "Do rocks come down only when it rains?"

"Mostly. This time the driver was just lucky. More than one wagon has gone over the side in a storm—mules, driver and all.

134

But not on a clear, dry day."

"So? Go on."

Cantwell shifted his rifle to a more offensive position. Rocklin hardly moved. If anything, he seemed to relax a little more. Cantwell, not getting the reaction he expected from the eastern mining engineer, said aggressively, "So if you know someone who wants my store, why don't you just come out and say so, instead of sicking a slick lawyer on me and then trying to pressure me in sneaky ways?"

"Why me?" Rocklin asked, showing no reaction at all to the insulting language and tone.

"I can add. I saw you with Leek this morning. You represent a mining company. Any outfit that moved into Sweetwater would need a store. And things have been happening. All since you showed up. Two and two. What about it?"

Rocklin considered, aware that he would have to take care what he said. "Tell me, Mr. Cantwell, did anyone suggest to you that it might be the mining company that is after your store?" There was the faintest flicker of surprise in the man's stony stare.

"I see," Rocklin said. "Well, Mr. Cantwell . . . I think there's only one thing I can say . . ."

"Say it."

"I strongly advise you not to sell your store to anyone."

"What?" Cantwell was taken completely by surprise.

"Not to anyone. And there's one more thing: I have heard there was some kind of trouble stirring long before I ever got to Sweetwater Valley."

Cantwell lowered his rifle and stood staring thoughtfully at Rocklin. Then he turned and slid the gun back in the saddle holster. "I remember the Lincoln County war," he said.

Rocklin nodded. "I believe a store fit some way into that mess." He mounted. "I want to get over the pass before dark. Coming?"

"Thanks. I would just as soon go over in the morning."

Rocklin started to ride away, then stopped and turned. "By the way, wasn't the other man a bit startled to see you step out from behind that rock with a gun?"

"What other man?"

Rocklin tensed and started to look up at the terrain above; then he thought better of it. Cantwell's expression was hard and alert.

"If you ride out the Jackson road to the east, where might you be going, besides over the pass," Rocklin asked.

"Nowhere," Cantwell snapped.

"A couple of hours ago there was a rider between you and me. Looked like a saddle tramp; dirty, unshaven. I watched both of you leave town." Cantwell started to turn. "I wouldn't look up at the peaks," Rocklin said.

"Not likely. I'm going to go on. There's a place to camp that nobody knows but me."

"I'll go along," Rocklin said.

"No need. I know this neck of the woods like the back of my hand. Drove freight over this road for five years before I bought my store. If some hired bushwhacker is out there, he's in bigger trouble than I am."

Rocklin started away again, and stopped again. "One more thing. You're an incautious man, Mr. Cantwell. If you do any more addition . . . Well, watch yourself."

Rocklin talked with Cantwell again in his store two days later, and several times after that, but neither man ever again mentioned the saddle tramp.

Chapter 10

It was the Laredo Kid who lit the fuse on the Sweetwater powder keg. Rocklin saw it happen. He wasn't ready for it but there was nothing he could do about it.

The Kid had been sulking around town off and on for three weeks, waiting for the time when Alex MacCrue would come back in, going over and over again in his mind the humiliation he had suffered, nursing his sick hatred. He had been drinking steadily, and despite his ready grin and exaggerated manners he was making the townspeople, who knew what he was up to, edgy.

He was sitting in the saloon slumped over a bottle when he glanced up and saw Jenny Lee riding out of town. Jenny Lee, who, pretty or not, had been a witness to, and maybe even a participant in, two of his defeats at the hands of MacCrue, the worst one being in the dining room when everyone, including MacCrue and Jenny, had ignored him, treating him like dirt. Even the banker and that strange nothing of a man who went around looking for gold or something were included in his fantasies of revenge. There was little that was specific about those fantasies; the Kid's mind was too disabled by a chaos of feelings to deal with specifics. There was no specific thought behind the impulse when he left his bottle on the table in the saloon, climbed aboard his horse and followed Jenny out of town. If the Kid had been capable of thought at that moment, he would have reflected that several people had surely seen Jenny ride out, and had just as surely seen him ride out in the same direction a bit later.

School was over when Jenny Lee went to the livery stable for her favorite horse and tried to ride away from a nagging restlessness and feeling of dissatisfaction. She too had been waiting for Alex MacCrue, impatiently. Some days before he had brought in the remains of her sister and brother-in-law, and had ridden to Jackson to order stones, assuring her that he would pick them up in a week or so. There had been an odd feeling of emptiness and anticlimax about the burial rites, and Jenny wanted to see the stones placed and have done with it, although she wouldn't have put it quite that way. Also, she simply wanted to see Alex MacCrue again. She wanted to find out if that moment of tenderness between them when Rocklin had brought the news of her sister had been real or imagined. Alex MacCrue had been all business since—helpful, considerate, but all business. She knew that something intangible but very important was taking place in her life, something crucial that would change everything, but she didn't know exactly what it was. And she didn't understand Alex MacCrue.

Jenny had left the road and was climbing toward a small rock formation just below the timberline, a favorite spot, warm and quiet, where she could sit and look out over the valley and listen to the trees. She paused for a moment to look back and saw the Laredo Kid riding quietly toward her. Instinctively, she glanced around to see if anyone was near, knowing that no one was. She had been going to dismount to sit on the massive old trunk of a fallen tree, one of the landmarks she enjoyed on this particular ride. Instead, she stayed on her horse and faced the Kid directly.

He was grinning, being, he thought, disarming. "Hello teacher," he said. The grin was not attractive, and Jenny made an effort to suppress a sudden anxiety.

"Hello." She smiled.

"Thought you might like some company."

"No, I really wouldn't. Not today. Thank you."

"Waiting for your boyfriend?"

Jenny nudged her horse forward, but the Laredo Kid blocked her off. She waited, looking squarely into his eyes, trying to make some contact. It was a mistake. There was no contact there to make. For the first time in her life Jenny looked into human eyes totally bereft of any kind of human reason, a killer's eyes. It frightened her terribly.

"I'm a better man than he is," the Kid said, edging his horse close. "Let me prove it. Ride up into the woods with me and let me prove it." Jenny struck at his face with her fist. He grabbed her horse's bridle and she struck at him again, lost her seat and fell, hitting her head on the old tree trunk.

The Kid started to dismount, but Jenny was lying still, momentarily dazed. Some urge to survive caused him to look around, but he saw no one. He looked back at Jenny, Sweetwater's schoolteacher, and stared at her. In the next instant he turned his horse and was gone. That was all.

But it was enough. Rocklin, five miles farther along on the road north and heading up toward the pass, could only watch. He had stopped and turned Buck around to check his back trail, although there was no special reason for him to do so except long habit and a vague

142

feeling that he was being watched, and he had seen the whole encounter through his glasses.

He watched, considering, as Jenny Lee stirred, sat on the log for a few minutes and then mounted to ride back toward town. She had been stunned for only a few seconds. Rocklin wondered whether he would have time to catch her before she reached town so he could ride in with her as if nothing had happened, see her home and return her horse to the stable. He knew it was unlikely. He also knew Jenny would probably ride back into town with her clothes soiled from her fall and a bad bruise on the right side of her head and her ear, and that she would be observed by the people who saw her ride out—and surely by the stableman.

The town would not take the brutalization of its schoolteacher lying down, but Rocklin was sure that, as was the way of towns, there would be talk before there was action. Probably some would even say that Jenny Lee had been asking for it for a long time, gallivanting around alone the way she did. But when Alex Mac-Crue heard about it, certainly when Jimmy rode home from school the next day at the latest, the fat would be in the fire.

Rocklin decided he had to hurry. It was essential that he have the documents that the stage driver had left for him at Old Lady Wells. On the downhill slope of the mountain desert pass he eased Buck into an easy but steady gallop. Two or three times he stopped to check his trail. The first time he did, he was sure he glimpsed a rider through the high outcroppings of rock near the pass, but later, when the trail descended into the desert with its wide open view, he saw nothing. It irritated him. He would have to take care on his way back to the valley, and he didn't have the time.

Whiskers welcomed Rocklin as an old buddy and demanded that he come in to sit and talk and have something to eat and drink.

"Got a package for you," he said. "Stage driver said you asked him to leave it here. What's the matter? Don't trust people in Sweetwater?"

"Sure I do," Rocklin said. "Just wanted a chance to ride down and listen to some more of your tall tales."

"Tall tales, huh? And I suppose that bundle of papers is nothing but assay reports?"

"You tell me. You looked through them, didn't you?"

"Course."

Rocklin laughed. The seal on the heavy envelope had not been broken. But, in fact, Rocklin had had an assay report included in the envelope, just in case the subject came up. He took it out and showed it to Whiskers, who glanced through it and then looked up in astonishment.

"Potash? Why that's just the wood ashes I

144

used to make lye out of for soap."

Rocklin nodded. "And spread over the ground before you turned it over for planting."

"Well, what in the sam hill . . ."

"Basically, the stuff they dig out of the ground is the same chemical. Potassium. But it's a different compound; it's mixed with different things. And you're exactly right. They use it to make soap; it's a big business. And someday there may be a big market for fertilizer."

Whiskers cackled delightedly. "Fertilizer! And what are they going to do with the stable shovelins? Are we all goin' to be up to our necks in horse manure?"

Rocklin enjoyed the sourdough and the coffee and the visit. But he had to cut it short.

He took care of Buck, slept a few hours and rolled out before dawn the next morning to find that Whiskers was already up and had coffee, salt pork and flapjacks ready. The talk at breakfast was lively and wide-ranging. Whiskers told Rocklin that he had first dug for gold, and found some too, after he had jumped ship in San Francisco in 1852 and headed for Hangtown. He had prospected all over the West and had got his share of the silver around Tombstone before buying Old Lady Wells "lock, stock and barrel."

"And what are you going to do when the stage stops running?" Rocklin asked. "It can't keep going much longer, can it?"

"Six months at the most," Whiskers said. "Only runnin' twice a month now, but I suppose you know that. Can't imagine why you came down this way 'stead of taking the Santa Fe down to Las Cruces, or even El Paso, and ridin' over. Would have saved you four days at least."

Rocklin laughed. "You surely are a nosy old coot. I just wanted to get the lay of the land before anyone knew what I was up to. You know how that is. But what are you going to do?"

"Oh, I'll be all right. I ain't broke. And I like this country."

"Wouldn't you like to be closer to town?"

"I don't know. Maybe, sometimes. But not too close, I'll tell you. Place like Sweetwater, a man can't scratch his back 'thout everybody wantin' to know about it."

"I'm thinking about buying, or building, a place in the valley. You could live on it. Look after it when I'm not there, which would be most of the time."

"I'll think about it," Whiskers said.

"I wish you would. Also . . ."

"Yep? Spit it out."

"The stage comes back by here in a day or two?"

"Yep."

"I'd be obliged if you would make sure something gets on it. Some papers. Confidential."

Whiskers eyed Rocklin for a moment. "Just who are you?"

Rocklin laughed. "I'm a mining engineer who lives in New York."

When Rocklin was mounted and ready to go he said, "Look, Whiskers, I wasn't sure I'd be in town when these reports came through and I didn't want them lying around loose. You see?"

"Sure, I see."

"I've got to go."

"Sure. Got to make sure that nobody jumps your potash claim."

"Take care of yourself."

"Yep. And Rocklin . . . well, did you get the idea somebody was comin' down the road behind you?" Rocklin waited. "Well, I haven't seen or heard him go by."

Rocklin nodded. He took off up the trail thinking that there was no place for several miles where anyone could surprise him, but when he got up near the pass he would have to leave it and circle around. And he had to be back in the valley in time to head off Alex MacCrue.

He got careless. He didn't take enough time scouting the rocks and trees. He moved too quickly from one cover to another without watching and listening long enough. He was aware that he was pressing his luck. He knew, and Buck knew, there was someone out there, but time was passing.

He was walking soundlessly and leading Buck when he heard a rifle being cocked behind him and slightly to his right. His duck to the left was so fast that the bullet barely brushed his hat. He yelped, as though hit, but he didn't stop; he stayed low and was twenty yards up the hill before echoes of the shot died. Then he waited. Half an hour later, when the bushwhacker edged cautiously out from behind the rock, Rocklin shot him. It was Jack Rooney.

When he reached Rooney, never taking his eyes off of him during his approach, the man was still alive. Rocklin kicked his rifle away and stood looking down at him, shaking his head. "Why?" he asked.

Rooney coughed and shook his head wearily. "I almost had it Rocklin. I had my hands on it. And you . . ."

"On what?"

"You again. That time before . . . I had it then too. A big piece of something good."

"You threw in with Belsher?"

"I'm dead, Rocklin. Because of you. I should have killed you as soon as I saw you, but I didn't know—"

"Who were you working for?"

"Rusty Mack."

"Mack? He's not in on it."

"He's a lost calf. I advised him to sell out and went after bigger stakes."

"But you told him what was going on."

"I told him nothing. By that time I had run into Belsher." He coughed again. "I could use some water, Rocklin."

"It would only prolong the agony. Why didn't Belsher just have you killed?"

"He threatened to. Knew him before, you know, up in Colorado some time back. Very mean man. Almost as mean as you. Gave me three choices. Get out, get shot or join him."

"Why didn't you tell him about me? He could easily have had me killed."

"Easily? Huh. I had a personal score to settle from the time before," Rooney said. "Now I'm dead."

"You're a fool, Rooney. You let him use you. You would have been dead anyway."

"A piece of the valley. I had my hands on it . . . aaah . . . I wish, I only wish I could live long enough to cut you into little pieces," Rooney gasped. Then he died.

Rocklin rode. When he came out of the pass into the valley, the sun was behind the tops of the mountains and the town of Sweetwater was still fifteen miles ahead. Rocklin pressed Buck into a full-out run and gave him his head. The horse loved it, but even so, Rocklin had to pull him back occasionally to let him walk and blow.

They were six miles from town when Rocklin saw a rider ahead, moving fast. They were less than two miles from town when Rocklin finally caught him. It was Alex MacCrue.

When MacCrue became aware of the rider behind him in the dark, he steered his horse off the road into a clump of trees, dismounted and waited. When the rider veered toward his hiding place, he took his rifle from the saddle holster and cocked it. He was pointing it at Rocklin when Rocklin pulled Buck to a stop and said, "MacCrue?"

"Who are you?" Alex demanded.

"Rocklin."

"What do you want?"

"They'll be waiting for you in town."

"What?"

"I said they'll be waiting for you in town. What have you done? What do you plan to do? You went to the Double B, didn't you, looking for Laredo?"

"I don't have time to talk to you, Rocklin." Alex started to mount, and Rocklin piled out of his saddle and pulled him down. Alex whirled on him, furious.

"This is none of your business, Rocklin. Now if you don't stay out of my way I'm going to have to whip you."

"Jenny Lee wasn't hurt badly. Are you listening? She fell off her horse and hit her head. I tell you it wasn't that bad. I saw it."

150

"You saw it and didn't stop it?" Alex pushed Rocklin away roughly and again started to mount. Rocklin pulled him down again.

"I couldn't. I was too far away. I saw it through my glasses. You've got to listen . . ." Alex knocked him down, and Rocklin thought the man must have hit him with a 20-pound boulder. He got up and pulled Alex from his saddle, and when Alex swung again Rocklin was ready for him. He tied him into a neat and sudden knot and put him on his back. He had him in a hand lock and his boot was pressing the side of his neck. Alex found he couldn't move without serious damage to muscles and tendons.

"Now listen, son," Rocklin said. "It's time you let your head rule your feelings for once, instead of the other way around. I need to talk to you, and you need to get control of yourself. They'll still be there, waiting for you, when we finish. Do you understand?" Alex nodded, glaring fire. Rocklin let up.

"All right. First, how do you know Laredo's in town?"

"Where else would he be? He's not at the ranch."

"You went to the ranch?"

"Yes."

"Was anyone there?"

"Two or three of the hands, that's all. If they're waiting to kill me, why didn't they do it at the ranch where no one would see them?"

"Good," Rocklin said. "You're thinking at least. Because they want people to see them. They'll be killing you in a fight you started over Jenny Lee, and not for some other reason that people might wonder about, such as trying to get their hands on your ranch. Understand?"

"No. Why me? Why my ranch? It's small potatoes compared to the other spreads."

"Don't know for sure. But a good guess is that Belsher somehow found out about your water."

Alex stared. "Who *are* you, Rocklin?"

"I don't have time . . ."

"That won't do. You know too much about my business. And everyone else's, it looks like. Why? What made you think I'd gone to the Double B?"

"All right. One of the things I was sent here for was to help clear up the trouble. And I know more about it than you do; you'll just have to take my word. I knew you had gone to the Double B because if you hadn't you would have been in town long before this."

Alex looked at Rocklin silently for a full minute. "How do you know Laredo's not in town?"

"Not a chance. They would probably stretch his neck. He took off like a scared jackrabbit."

"What should I do?"

"Just what you were going to do. Go into

town, into the saloon, looking for Laredo. But wait for me to get there. I'll be having a quiet drink at the table in the back. Nobody will take much notice of me." Alex mounted. "And one other thing. At one point I want you to say that you know where the missing cattle are, and you're going after them tomorrow. Blurt it out. Understand?"

"But . . . but I can't! I mean . . . well, nobody would believe me!"

"You mean you don't think you could be a convincing liar."

"Well, put it any way you want to, Rocklin. The fact is that it just plain wouldn't work."

"All right. The cattle are in a high valley not far south from the cave. A hidden mountain valley. Do you know where I mean?"

"Sure but . . . I've never even been in there. There's no way to get cattle in."

"Yes there is. One cow at a time, on the desert side. I've seen them, MacCrue, and you will be going after them. You and Jimmy and I. So you don't have to be a good liar. Will you do it?"

"You're crazy, man. They'll walk right into my ranch."

"No. They'll be too busy. Besides, they still don't know who you have helping you. Or how many. Will you do it?"

"All right. I'll try."

"Good. And control your temper. You'll

153

need all your wits about you."

When the Laredo Kid went back to the Double B after accosting Jenny Lee, he rode into the yard at a run and went directly into the big house. Ed Belsher glanced up from his desk, read the Kid's face and said, "What's the matter?" The Kid didn't answer at once and Belsher got up and walked toward him threateningly. "I said what's the matter." The Kid told him. Belsher's neck and face puffed up frighteningly. The whites of his eyes turned red.

"Oh you dirty —" He almost choked. He knocked the Kid down and kicked him. "You stupid . . ." He kicked again and the Kid covered his head with his arms and rolled up into a ball. Belsher felt himself getting dizzy and fought for control. "We're almost there and you . . . almost there and you have to go sniffing after the schoolteacher like a dog. Get up! Get up!" He went back to his desk and sat down. He was almost gasping.

The Kid stood and looked at the floor. "I'd better . . ."

"Yes, you'd better. You'd better get out. You're no good to me now. Get out! Wait. Where are you going?"

"I don't know. I thought . . . El Paso, maybe."

154

"No, you damn fool. I want you out of circulation completely. Wait. Go down to the line shack at hidden valley. And get out of those stupid clothes. Anybody can spot you ten miles away. Change and go. Now."

Belsher sat for a long time, staring out the window of the spacious office, drumming his fingers on the desk. Finally, he got up and told the guard at the front door to bring him a horse.

"Who's up at the lookout?" he asked the guard as he was ready to ride.

"Corky."

"Are the Hammer twins around?"

"Yeah. Down at the corral."

"Tell them to stay close. I may need them."

The lookout was on the crest of one of the foothills that stretched between the Double B and MacCrue's place. The two ranch houses were not far apart, and from the lookout there was a clear view of the entrance to Alex's canyon, but not the canyon itself. The man stationed there came alert when he heard someone coming, and was surprised to see that it was Belsher. He was using his glasses when Belsher came up the last rise in the trail.

"Hello, Mister Belsher," he said.

"Anyone been in or out?" Belsher asked.

"Only the kid. Rode in from school a couple of hours ago."

"You sure? No one else?"

"Nope."

Belsher shook his head. "Who in the hell have they got in there?"

"Beats me."

"You were there that night?"

"Yup."

"Was there more than one man firing at you?"

"Could have been three or four. But I have a feeling there was only one. If so, that one is enough."

"They don't go anywhere at night?" Belsher asked.

The man shrugged. "Not that I can see in the dark."

"Well, if Alex MacCrue heads out at any time, I want to know. Pronto. Understand?"

"Yup."

"I mean right then. Signal the house."

"Yup."

"And if MacCrue hasn't shown his face by the time the kid rides past on his way home from school tomorrow, I want to know right then. You got that?"

"Yup."

"Right then. It's important."

"You'll know."

"Good. We'll be riding into town right then. And if MacCrue rides into my place, he'll be told that we're all in town."

"You mean you expect MacCrue to come

156

riding in here tomorrow afternoon?"

"Right. And if he does, let him come in. He'll be told we're in town, and he'll follow."

Corky looked at Belsher dubiously. "You're the boss."

Belsher was sitting at a table by himself and the Double B men were lined up at the bar when Alex MacCrue walked in. No one at the bar as much as glanced his way, and MacCrue knew at once that Rocklin had been right. They had been waiting for him. He looked at each man in turn, noticed Rocklin at the back table, and walked over to where Belsher was sitting. "Were's the Laredo Kid?" he demanded.

Rocklin shifted in his chair for a straight-on view down the scruffy bar and for easier access to the gun under his coat. He was not feeling cheerful. To him, violence in a closed, dark place with men stumbling all over themselves was no way to run a railroad. Already the room was steamy and reeking with cheap whisky, acrid tobacco smoke and sweaty men, tense men who were waiting for something to happen. And it was not too clean. The sawdust was stained here and there with tobacco spit, the tables were old and scarred and wobbly and most of the chairs were held together with bailing wire. It was a miserable place to die.

"Why, I don't know," Belsher said mildly.

"He rode out a couple of days ago. Said something about El Paso."

"Aren't you his boss? Doesn't he do just what you tell him to do?"

Belsher tensed and his neck swelled. The implication of MacCrue's question was clear to everyone, even though Jenny Lee's name had not been mentioned — and wouldn't be.

"Get a gun, MacCrue," Belsher said.

The door of the saloon swung open and Hendryx walked in with the gunman he had hired. Brennan, whose place was just north of the Double H, was with them. The barman gave Hendryx a bottle and glasses and the three men took one of the two remaining tables. Hendryx, who was within reaching distance of Belsher, nodded to him and Belsher nodded back. Rocklin shifted his chair a little more, feeling more pessimistic than ever.

"Maybe the Kid rode up to the hidden valley," MacCrue said. "I know where it is. I can always go up after him. And when I'm there I might just bring back the missing cattle. Tomorrow."

Both Hendryx and Brennan started to say something, but Belsher's furious rasp cut them off. "Get a gun. Give him a gun, Nate."

Nathaniel Hammer, one of the giant twins, offered his gun to MacCrue, butt first.

"What's the matter, Belsher," MacCrue prodded, "do you have to have a gun in your hand before you're a man?"

Ezekial Hammer, called Zeke, turned suddenly away from the bar, bumping into Mac-Crue, almost sending him sprawling. "Why don't you look where you headed?" Zeke demanded. He took off his gun belt and laid it on the bar. "See. I don't have a gun. Am I a man?" Both twins were grinning with a kind of evil glee.

Alex nodded slightly. So this was it. Both men had killed with their hands. Twice. And they enjoyed it. 'Before Zeke even knew the fight had started, MacCrue hit him in the mouth with all his strength. Zeke staggered back, spitting blood, then came casually for his prey. The men at the bar shifted toward the front of the room. Tables and chairs scraped back. Rocklin didn't move.

Zeke suddenly charged. He swung a wild right at MacCrue's face and missed and then caught him with a left on his rib cage. Mac-Crue went flying and caught himself on the bar. He knew what he was up against now. He was in bad trouble. The blow on his side had almost made his knees turn to water. Zeke aimed at his face again, twice, and missed, and Alex realized that as long as he stayed conscious, Zeke could never hit him there.

The fight quickly settled into a kind of routine. Every time Zeke swung at Alex's head, Alex battered at his mouth and nose and eyes.

But when the giant came at him with his enraged lunge, Alex was hurt and sent sprawling. Time and again, Zeke tried to lock him in a bear hug, but Alex knew he had to avoid that if he wanted to come out alive. Alex, dodging and ducking, tried body blows, a kidney punch, a rabbit punch, and the brute didn't even notice them. His face was bruised and bloody and he just grinned and kept pressing in.

It seemed to Alex that he had been fighting for hours, and was about finished, when he caught a wild blow on his shoulder and went sprawling the length of the bar, right at Rocklin's feet. Zeke wiped the blood from his mouth, turned to the bar and demanded a bottle.

"Stay down a minute," Rocklin said in a conversational tone. "He figures he's got you."

"So do I," Alex said.

"Don't hurry," Rocklin said. "It's intermission." He was right. Every man in the saloon was pouring a drink. Or two drinks. They knew it was all over and that Zeke would break Alex MacCrue's back.

"He lumbers in like a bear, wide open," Rocklin said. "The next time he does it, flatten your hand out stiff, like the end of a board, and jab him as hard as you can just below his Adam's apple."

"What?"

"He's ready, now. Use your hand like the end of a board, and jab him in the throat with your fingers as hard as you can, right below his Adam's apple."

"It better work," Alex muttered. He got to his feet, and the men in the saloon, who had been watching the giant, turned their eyes toward him. Their faces were expressionless. Not a man in the room, except Belsher, particularly liked what was happening. The Hammer bullies were not popular.

Alex didn't wait. He moved forward slowly in a crouch. Zeke grinned at him, took another swallow of whisky, and rushed, just like a grizzly. Alex jabbed him hard in the throat. The brute stepped back, taken by surprise. He made a terrible rasping gasp trying to suck air through his crushed windpipe, staggered and fell to the floor.

The men in the saloon couldn't believe it. They stared at Zeke, and then they stared at Alex. There was a moment of complete silence. Then Nate Hammer said, "Now it's my turn."

Alex went into his crouch and moved slowly forward. Nate circled warily. Some of the men moved as though to intervene.

"Let them be," Belsher said through his teeth.

Hendryx took his gun out and stuck it in Belsher's back. "Call him off," he said quietly, "or I'll kill you where you sit."

Alex and Nate were still circling.

"That's enough, Nate," Belsher yelled. Nate paid no attention.

Hendryx prodded Belsher with his .45. "Stop him." Belsher got up and took Nate's arm, but Nate brushed him off. Belsher took his arm again. "No," he insisted.

"You have no right," Nate said.

"As long as you're working for me, you'll take my orders," Belsher said, and then in a lower voice, "Later you fool. Later. Understand?"

While they were arguing, Zeke Hammer lay on the floor, struggled for air, lost consciousness and died.

"Leave," Rocklin said to Alex. "I'll see you at your place."

While Belsher argued with Nate, Alex walked out, the men in the saloon moving aside to give him room. The quiet argument was still going on a few minutes later when Rocklin brushed past the men and almost unnoticed, made his way to the door.

"It's not over yet," Belsher was telling Nate. "You can have Alex MacCrue when it is. I promise you."

"When?" Nate demanded.

"Soon. Now take your brother home. It's all over for tonight." He turned to his men. "All right, get him up and put him on his horse."

Two men reached for Zeke's arms to pull him

162

erect, and dropped him at once.

"Well?" Belsher demanded.

"He's dead," one of the men said.

"Dead?" Belsher asked.

Nate pushed through and stared down at his brother, not believing it. His mouth was hanging open and he was shaking his head slowly, as though trying to grasp the situation. Suddenly, he went for the door, knocking three men down who were standing in his path. Another man, a gunman Belsher had imported and who hated and feared the twins and had been waiting for just such an opportunity, gave the giant a hard shoulder rather than be pushed out of the way. Nate Hammer, blind with rage, whirled and pulled his gun, and was shot dead.

Chapter 11

When Rocklin left the saloon he went to his room at the hotel to pick up the documents Whiskers had saved for him. He left the town the back way and hit the road running so he could put some distance between him and the town before Belsher and his outfit started home.

When he reached the entrance to MacCrue's canyon, slipping in behind a small rise to the south, instead of coming in from the road where he could be seen, Jimmy challenged him from behind a rock.

"It's all right, Jimmy," Rocklin told him. "Come on up to the house. Your brother's going to need you."

"Leave my lookout?" Jimmy asked.

"It's all right. Nobody's going to come in

165

tonight. Come on."

Alex was lying down when they arrived at the ranch house.

"What's the matter, Alex? What happened?" Jimmy asked.

"You don't look so well," Rocklin said. "Do you have some liniment?"

"Of course I have liniment," Alex said, sounding cranky. "And why shouldn't I look well?"

"Is anything broken?" Rocklin asked.

"No."

"I'll get the liniment," Jimmy said. "What happened?"

"Your brother beat up one of the Hammer twins," Rocklin told him.

Jimmy stared at Rocklin a moment, clearly skeptical, and then said to Alex, "You did?"

"More the other way around." Alex said.

"I'll heat some beef broth," Rocklin said. "What else do you want?"

"Nothing."

"You'll need something. You can get three or four hours sleep, then we have to go."

"Go where?"

"To the hidden valley. They'll be heading there, and it's a perfect chance to cut down the odds."

Alex lay back, exhausted. "I hope you know what we're doing," he said.

When Alex and Jimmy were asleep, Rocklin rode out to the rock with the fissure where Laredo had stashed the money from the stage robbery. He took it out and put the copies of the documents from Sante Fe in its place.

Jimmy woke with a start when Rocklin returned. "What's that?" he asked.

"The bank money from the stage robbery."

"You robbed the stage?"

"Don't wake your brother. The Laredo Kid robbed the stage. Then he hid the money in a rock up on the north wall of your canyon."

"Why?"

"To implicate your brother. Make it look as though Alex had done it."

"When?"

"When you and Alex were up in the cave."

"What are you going to do with the money?"

"Return it. That is, Alex is going to return it. Go to sleep."

"Tell me about Dunbar," Rocklin asked.

"I don't know a lot," Alex said, "except what I heard my pa say." He groaned as he pulled a buckskin shirt over his head. "Are you sure we have to do this?"

"I'm sure. My guess is that they'll be riding early, before sun-up. Belsher knows that you know. When you mentioned the hidden valley, that was it."

"But he knows his men can shoot me before I can get near the place."

"He doesn't want that, now. Hendryx and Brennan both heard you say it. And Belsher still doesn't know who's working for you. What about Dunbar? Did he have any other spread around here?"

"Another spread? Not that I've ever heard of."

"I've heard his place was called Star Ranch before he died and before Belsher bought it."

Alex nodded. "Dunbar married an Apache squaw. Her name was Morning Star, or something like that. I heard it said that she was the best cook in the valley. Old Dunbar doted on her. He called his place Star's ranch, and I guess the name stuck. He even used a star brand for awhile."

"Oh? What was his original brand? Was it the Lazy D?"

"How did you know?"

"I just now made the connection. Of course. Belsher was planning to fence half the valley off, not to mention some open range."

"Barbed wire?"

"Almost certainly. I saw fifty tons of it sitting on a freight dock in Las Vegas. It was consigned to the Lazy D. He's desperate,

MacCrue, and he won't stop at anything. Can you make it?"

Alex stretched. He felt as if he had been stomped by a horse.

"I can make it." He finished dressing, not bothering to suppress his grunts and groans as he pulled on his pants and boots.

"You'll need a gun," Rocklin told him. Alex merely nodded and took a holster, cartridge belt and Colt .45 from a cabinet. Jimmy appeared from his room upstairs, all ready to go, carrying a rifle.

"You're not going," Alex told him, astonished.

"Why not? I can shoot. I'm near as good as you are. And I'm near as old as you were when you took over the ranch."

"I had no choice. You do. You're not going."

"He could stay out of sight," Rocklin said, "and cover us."

"You stay out of this," Alex said. "He's already been nearly killed. And by the way, since you seem to know everything, who shot him?"

Rocklin shrugged. "I don't know. Probably Laredo. He's the one who stashed the bank money when he knew you were both gone."

Jimmy had told Alex about the bank money as soon as he woke up.

"I don't understand why you took it out," Alex said.

"I put something in its place. Copies of records — deeds and applications for government land — that show what Belsher has been up to."

When Alex had considered this he said, "A neat trap."

"If it works," Rocklin said.

"It will have to, the way we're forcing his hand, won't it?"

"A hundred things could go wrong," Rocklin said. " 'The best laid plans of mice and men gang aft agley.' "

Alex stared at him. "And he quotes Burns, too."

"I'd like to be out there when they ride south," Rocklin said. "Just to be sure they're doing what I expect them to do."

"We're not going to follow them, are we?"

"No. We'll ride north, take the road. You and Jimmy . . ."

"Jimmy's not going."

"I am going," Jimmy said.

"What's the matter with you Rocklin? You know it's too risky."

"I'm going," Jimmy insisted.

"He could stay out of sight," Rocklin said. "Wouldn't you feel better if you knew he was behind you?"

"No."

"And maybe he's earned the right. Think how you would feel. Think how you felt at his age."

"Do you have any children, Rocklin?" Alex demanded.

"Yes. A boy and a girl. And I'd be pleased to think that my boy was a little bit like Jimmy."

"Why will we ride north?" Alex asked.

"I'll tell you on the way. We ought to get going. Oh, and I need a candle." Alex, looking resentful, didn't bother to ask why.

They were out of sight behind the big rock when Belsher's men, six of them, rode by a mile or so away.

"I would like to see the lookout's face when he sees us ride north," Rocklin said.

"What lookout?" Jimmy asked. "How do you know there's a lookout?"

"They're always watching, whenever they can see anything," Rocklin told the boy, "from up on that hill, the one that peaks. See? Ever since the night I fired on them. And I've visited Belsher at his ranch."

"You get around," Alex grumbled.

"I've visited all the ranches," Rocklin said. "I wanted people to get used to me so my wandering around wouldn't worry them."

"And to create a mystery?" Alex asked. It

obviously rankled him that he himself had been somewhat misled about Rocklin.

"I have to appear to be doing something else besides what I am doing," Rocklin said mildly, "or I would soon be dead."

"All right," Alex said, "I want to know the plan. Right now."

Rocklin told him. Alex and Jimmy would take an old unused trail that cut east from the stage road near the summit and then turned south and followed the desert side of the mountains until it sloped into the semi-desert grassland. The old trail would eventually meet the southern trail out of the valley that Belsher's men were taking, but some distance south of the hidden valley. Even with the hard descent from the stage road, Alex and Jimmy should approach the entrance to the hidden valley long before Belsher's men did.

"The lookouts—there are two of them—won't be expecting you from that direction at all. Walk in quietly, take cover in the rocks just north of the entrance, and wait. Are you sure you know where the entrance is from my description?"

"I'm sure," Alex said. "I would never have believed it, but I'm sure. What are you going to do?"

"I'm going to take the old game trail down

172

the west side of the mountain. There is a hole through the rocks there, a watercourse. It's just big enough for a man to crawl through, and it will take me right into the valley. I've been there before. The lookouts won't even know I'm there until it's too late."

"The candle," Alex said.

"Right."

"I don't want any unnecessary killing," Alex warned.

Rocklin eyed him. "I won't do anything unnecessary. But there can't be anyone behind us when the riders get there."

"Knock them out with one of your trick punches," Alex said, and it was clear from the way he said it that trick punches left a bad taste in his mouth.

Rocklin just looked at him shaking his head. "Every man is different. You can't be certain. A blow that would kill one man might just put another one out for a few minutes." He turned abruptly away, stopped and said, "No shooting. Wait for me," and was gone.

Rocklin would also have liked to see Belsher's face when the lookout brought the news that three men had ridden out of MacCrue's place going north.

"North!" Belsher yelled. "What the hell for?" The cowhand didn't answer. "He was bluffing!" Belsher said. "He doesn't know where the cattle are at all." But he thought this over and knew it wouldn't do.

The ranch hand, who had grown up in Sweetwater, said, "There's another way . . ."

"Shut up!" Belsher said. He was scowling. "They're trying to put us off the track. They have more men who will be riding south."

"Why?" the hired hand asked.

Belsher scowled and muttered and waved it away. "What did you say about another way?"

"There's an old desert trail down the other side of the mountains. If MacCrue knows where the place is, he'll get there first."

"Can they sneak up on the sentries from that direction?" Belsher asked.

"Not a chance."

"Then what good will it do them?" Belsher yelled.

Rocklin took his time down the mountain trail. His was the shortest route to the little valley and he was not worried about being late. He knew his approach to the entrance from the back way would have to be slow and easy, even though the men on guard wouldn't have the faintest thought of being surprised from the rear.

He gave no thought to the tunnel, to the dead snake or anything else he might encounter, he just told Buck to wait, lit the candle and crawled into it. The going turned out to be easy, and Rocklin had entered the grassy valley while Alex and Jimmy were still several miles away.

He didn't try to cross it, but worked his way around the edge, crawling much of the way and walking only when there was sufficient cover. It took him two hours. Near the line shack, he stood in the shadow of a rock for half an hour before he located the two sentries. The first one was easy. Rocklin spotted the glow of the man's cigarette almost at once, high and to his left, on the north side of the entrance. It was different with the man on the south side. He was concealed by rocks all around him and Rocklin had to wait until he stirred. Finally, the man got up and stretched and lit a smoke.

Rocklin decided to take the man on the highest ground first, figuring that the one at the lower level would be more likely to be looking down at the trail than up at his partner. He had just started to move when somebody inside the shack, not more than thirty yards away, stirred and yawned and rolled out

175

of a creaky bunk.

Rocklin froze. Three men. Well, he thought, first things first. He waited, and was in luck. The man came out of the shack, stretched noisily and looked at the sky, calculating the time. He was lighting a cigarette when Rocklin, with the least possible fuss, stunned him and dragged him behind a rock, deploring the foolishness of his own sentiment. There was plenty of rope in the shack, and Rocklin took a length of it and hog-tied the man. The man came around before he was finished, and Rocklin whispered, "Make a sound and I'll kill you."

"The only sensible thing would be to kill you," Rocklin said softly as he put a loop over the man's head and secured it in a clever way to his feet. The man's eyes bulged a little and Rocklin gave him a little more slack. "Now," he said, "if you relax as much as you can, don't struggle, don't even move or talk, you won't choke yourself to death." The man looked a pleading question at him and Rocklin said, "I'll be back."

It took Rocklin another half an hour to reach the man on the high rock without alerting him, and even so, at one point, when Rocklin dislodged a small rock, the man called, "Laredo?" From the other side of the entrance came the sour answer: "Shut up."

176

Rocklin left the man thoroughly immobilized, and even unable to speak above a raspy whisper, and started down toward Laredo. Laredo, on edge and still smoldering, still plotting his revenge on Alex MacCrue, turned at the last second and shied as Rocklin chopped at the vulnerable muscle below his ear. He pulled violently away, reaching for his gun, lost his footing on the edge of a shallow precipice and went over. Rocklin watched him for ten minutes, but he didn't move. Then he tried to find a way down to the Kid, but could not.

Rocklin was disgusted with himself. He could have killed the Kid quietly and easily with his knife, but now the gunman was a loose end and a potential danger — he might well be alive. It hadn't been a long fall, and his gun was lying near him. Rocklin had ignored his one favorite dictum for such an operation: Fools don't live long.

When he reached the desert entrance to the hidden valley, Rocklin stepped into the open and waved at the north trail. Soon, Alex and Jimmy joined him. He told them about Laredo.

"It will be a couple of hours before they get here," Alex said. "What should we do?"

Rocklin shrugged. "Find a comfortable place where we can rest and see him at the same time, and wait. He might be dead. But we can't chance it."

"Then, when Belsher's men get here, we can leave Jimmy to watch him," Alex said.

"Jimmy will have to shoot him if he moves," Rocklin said, and Alex nodded.

"I can do it," Jimmy declared.

"Let's hope you won't have to," his brother said. He turned to Rocklin. "What will we do when they come, start shooting?"

Rocklin tried to judge the flavor of his question. Was it sarcastic? He decided it wasn't. Anyway, he thought, it had better not be. If Alex wasn't in this all the way, they might all be dead by morning. And the time was three o'clock.

"No." Rocklin said. "It's too risky. We don't know how the light will be, and if we just start shooting they'll dive for cover, which there's plenty of, and we might never get them out. We'll have to confront them, close up. They'll be surprised and won't know what to think. And if we don't actually have our guns in our hands, they'll wonder how many men we have hiding behind rocks. It will make them cautious."

"And if they decide we don't have anyone?" Alex asked.

Rocklin said, "At six against two they might get overconfident."

It was a longer wait than they thought it would be. When they saw the riders coming, Alex sent Jimmy to a spot they had chosen that overlooked both the trail and the Laredo Kid.

The sun was well up when Belsher's riders wheeled their mounts away from the desert trail and headed toward the hidden entrance to the trail that led up to the valley.

The men, obviously gunmen and not cowhands, were certainly surprised when Rocklin and Alex MacCrue stepped out in front of them. They pulled up and stared. One of them said, "What in hell?" Another said, "MacCrue? What do you think you're up to?" When neither MacCrue nor Rocklin answered at once, the men looked around, shifting in their saddles. "What's the prospector doing here?" one of them asked. "Who else is with you?"

"It's all over for Belsher," Alex said. "You men only ride for him. Is it going to be worth it to go to prison for murder?"

"What's your stake in this?" the man asked Rocklin. He got no reply. "Well, what are you going to do?" he demanded of Alex.

"What I said. Take the cattle in." Alex replied.

"You're plumb loco! It'll take a week. You can only get them out of there one or two at a time. And what do you expect us to do, help?"

"A lot of good you would be," Alex said. "Be smart. Ride into Jackson and tell what you know about Belsher. It'll go easier for all of you."

"Loco," the man said. A thought occurred to him. "Where's Art and Tex and Laredo?"

"What difference does it make?" Alex asked. "You can see they're not here."

Up behind his rock, Jimmy, engrossed in the strange scene below, caught a movement from the corner of his eye, whirled to his right and threw a shot at Laredo just as the Kid, staring down at Alex, was about to shoot him in the back. Laredo's shot went wild, as he flinched from a searing pain in his shoulder, lost his footing and rolled the rest of the way down the rocky decline to the desert floor.

One of the riders facing Rocklin and Alex went for his gun, and then the others did. There was a wild burst of gunfire as Rocklin and Alex pulled iron. It lasted five seconds, no more. When it was over the six gunslingers were dead. Four of them were already on the ground, and two were slowly crumpling.

Rocklin turned slowly to Alex. "You got four of them," he said. "Fanning a gun. I don't believe it."

"Jimmy helped me with one, and you helped me with one," Alex said. "I don't believe you. What are you anyway?"

Jimmy scrambled down from the rocks. He was hyper. "We got them all, we got them all," he jabbered. Then he looked at the dead men and tried not to be sick.

"Where's Laredo?" Rocklin asked.

"I hit him," Jimmy said, "but not very hard, I think. I wasn't watching him," he admitted.

"Where was he the last time you saw him?" Rocklin insisted.

Jimmy pointed. "Right over there." They looked. There was no Laredo Kid.

Alex looked at Rocklin. "I'm sorry," he said. "I shouldn't have said what I did about unnecessary killing."

"Let's get out of the open," Rocklin said. "I doubt that he could get back up that cliff, and apparently he's lost his six-shooter."

"He dropped it when he went over. I saw him," Jimmy said.

"But the horses have scattered," Rocklin said. "If he caught one of them he's got a rifle. Get down."

At that precise second, a bullet crashed and whistled off the rock just above their heads.

"I'll get you, Alex MacCrue," Laredo screamed. "I'll get you! I'll get you!" Then there were hoofbeats that quickly faded to the south.

Rocklin was quiet, frowning thoughtfully. Jimmy was white around the lips. The three listened awhile. "Is it a trick?" Alex asked.

Rocklin shook his head slowly. "I don't think so. I didn't like the sound of that threat."

"Neither did I," Alex said. He studied Rocklin's face.

"You think he'll hit the ranch?"

"Maybe," Rocklin said, meeting Alex's eyes.

Alex paled. "Jenny," he said.

"Maybe."

"I'm going after him. Now," Alex said, and started for his horse.

"Wait a minute," Rocklin said. "It's 35 miles to town, at least, the way he's going. It's 25 by the desert trail and the stage road. That way, Jimmy can go with you and you can take an extra horse apiece."

"I won't ride a Double B horse. Our horses are all right," Alex said.

"Suit yourself," Rocklin said.

"I'm not just being stiff-necked," Alex said. "If by any chance any of Belsher's riders caught us with his horses they would hang us on the spot. Besides, where did we get them?"

"It's a good point," Rocklin said. "Anyhow,

I've got to go back the way I came because I left my horse. I'll be back at the ranch long before Laredo is up that way, just in case."

"All right," Alex said, "but we're leaving now."

Rocklin had a thought. "Wait. Jimmy isn't going into town with you, is he?"

"Of course not. He's going back to the ranch, and by the back way."

"Good. Then there's no need for me right now. I have some unfinished business. I'll see you later."

"Suit yourself," Alex said.

Rocklin turned and patted the boy on the shoulder. "You did fine, Jim. I'm glad you were along."

Alex looked embarrassed, as though Rocklin had complimented him. "He's the best," he said. "Come on, Jimmy."

Rocklin untied the man on the high point first. His face was slightly blue, but the color came back as soon as he got to his feet. He stumbled but went willingly when Rocklin urged him down through the rocks to the shack. The other man stomped around to get his circulation going after Rocklin untied him and then asked, "What was the shooting?"

"Six of your friends are dead," Rocklin told

him. "And both of you will be too unless you are smart enough to get out. Now. Ride east. Those are your choices."

The men looked Rocklin up and down, wondering where his gun was, and then looked at each other. It was obvious to Rocklin that they were just cowpokes doing a job, not gunmen, and both were quite young. It was also obvious that they were thinking of the two-to-one odds, even though their own guns were in the shack where Rocklin had tossed them earlier.

"What friends?" the curious cowpoke asked.

"Belsher's men."

"Belsher? We don't work for Belsher. We work for Purley White. And who the hell are you?"

"Two choices," Rocklin said. "What's it going to be?"

"Who's with you?" They asked in unison.

"Nobody."

The men rushed him. But they were stiff and not too fast. In an instant, one was doubled up on the ground hugging his solar plexus and trying to get his breath and the other was sprawled a few feet away with a painfully wrenched arm and shoulder. Rocklin waited patiently for them to collect themselves, and when they were sitting looking at him, asked, "Is that your choice? You'd rather die than throw in a bad hand?"

The young men got to their feet, glancing at each other and wondering if they had an acceptable way out.

"Are you friends?" Rocklin asked. They nodded. "Which one's Tex and which Art?" The men only stared. "Where are you from?"

"Texas." One of them said.

"Good. You can be there in three or four hours. It's all over here, anyway. Do you see any point in staying? Do you have your gear here?" Rocklin waited, not wanting to press too hard.

Finally one of the men looked at his buddy. "I'd just as soon go home for a visit," he said. It was all his friend was waiting for, but he wanted the last word, or at least the next to last.

"I've got pay coming," he told Rocklin, and his buddy was quick to pick it up.

"So have I."

"How much?" Rocklin asked.

"About twenty dollars."

"Me too."

Rocklin took out his wallet, extracted forty dollars in green-backs and handed them to the men. They stared at him in astonishment. The wallet was fat. They looked at each other; they glanced around; they looked at

Rocklin again.

"It's legal tender," Rocklin said. "You can exchange it for coin at any bank in the land."

"What are you going to tell anyone who asks?" one of the men said.

"Absolutely nothing. Neither are you. Are we in agreement?"

"Who *are* you?"

"You'll ride straight out and not look back? Don't go south at all. You might run into men coming this way, and they might get the wrong idea. The safest way is straight east. Agreed?" The young men nodded. "Good. There's one thing you can do, though; you can help me get the bodies together and covered."

Rocklin took his last trip through the high rim of the little valley, emerging from the tunnel with a feeling of accomplishment and relief. He noticed that it was a fine warm day. "Well, that's over," he told Buck. "We'll be heading home pretty soon." The horse tossed his head and snorted. He was glad to see Rocklin but he had to grumble a little at being left standing so long.

Rocklin stretched thoroughly and realized he was very tired. He gave Buck some sugar from the saddle bags. "One more chore before we get some rest," he said.

He found Rooney's body easily enough, a little the worse for wear from animal life, but Rooney's horse had not stayed ground-hitched very well. An hour went by before Rocklin found the horse and tied the body onto the saddle.

He found the route he had first taken through the high woods down the west side of Sweetwater Valley and followed it to the faint trail that twisted down toward Belsher's place, the Double B—and before that Star's Ranch and before that the Lazy D. He led the horse with Rooney's body down the trail as far as he dared, as close to the ranch as he could get, gave it a smack on the flank and watched it disappear with its surprise package for Belsher.

It was a good three hours before Rocklin got Buck to the livery stable, rubbed down and fed, and was headed for his bed in the hotel. He went up the back way to his room, thinking that the town seemed unusually quiet for a Saturday evening. A few minutes later he was dead to the world and didn't even hear the Laredo Kid's last gunshots.

Chapter 12

At just about the time that Alex and Jimmy were heading up the desert trail toward the stage road, Jenny Lee was having her usual Saturday breakfast at the hotel.

She was sitting at a table with banker Higgins, who was drawing her into the kind of small talk considered fitting during a meal. In fact, the banker seemed to be avoiding saying anything interesting, which added to Jenny's impatience and mental turmoil. She had heard nothing from Alex MacCrue, not even since her encounter with the Laredo Kid, and she knew the incident was causing considerable talk around town, and therefore, probably, the valley. She had even heard one of the boys telling Jimmy MacCrue about it at school on Friday.

It bothered her very much to see her students

stop talking when she approached in the schoolyard, and when she saw the people in town react in the same way, she was embarrassed and irritated. She reflected that it had been heedless of her to ride directly into town, furious and slightly disheveled, after the incident, and that embarrassed her even more. If she had had any sense, she told herself, she would have gone quietly home the back way and composed herself before riding to the stable, and nobody would have been the wiser.

She even thought that some people glanced at her in a disapproving and perhaps a malicious way. She had no way of knowing that the town's sentiment was overwhelmingly in her favor, or that the town, like Jenny herself — whether she knew it or not — was waiting to see what Alex MacCrue was going to do.

And this morning on her way to breakfast — when she had actually said to herself, "Where is he?" — it seemed to her that the glances of people she met on the little street had been even more skittish than they had been the day before. And Mr. Higgins prattled on.

Finally she couldn't stand any more. "What is it, Mr. Higgins?" she demanded.

Mr. Higgins was taken aback. "I don't know what you mean, my dear."

"You do know what I mean. And why am I suddenly 'my dear' instead of 'Miss Lee'? I insist that you tell me."

Higgins looked pained. "Over coffee perhaps?"

"Now," Jenny said, and Higgins reflected, not without a touch of his own peculiar humor, that the schoolmarm's way with recalcitrant children was well-known in the valley.

"Alex MacCrue was in town last night looking for the Laredo Kid," Higgins said soothingly.

Jenny's jaw almost dropped in a most unladylike way, and then two pink spots of color appeared high on her cheeks. "How odd that I seem to be the last to know of Mr. MacCrue's gallantry," she said sweetly. She was furious.

Higgins suppressed a smile. "Well, uh, it seems that 'the Kid' " — Higgins made a wry face — "wasn't here, but half of Mr. Belsher's gang was. In the saloon."

As quickly as Jenny's cheeks had turned pink, they turned pale.

"Is he all right?" she asked quickly. It was indiscreet, but she didn't care.

"Apparently so. I gather he was badly battered, and in no condition to go . . . uh, visiting, but he got on his horse and rode home; at least, he rode in that direction."

"Battered?"

"Yes. Well, it seems he ran afoul of a brute named Zeke Hammer. You have heard of the Hammer twins?"

Jenny was ashen. "Mr. Higgins, I ought to

go to him."

"I understand how you feel," Higgins said, and through her fear Jenny saw that he really did. "But there is talk today — I don't know its source — that MacCrue left his ranch last night. Or early this morning."

"I don't understand."

"Apparently, he had his reasons."

Jenny didn't know what to say. Higgins cleared his throat.

"What else?" Jenny asked.

"It appears," Higgins said, "that Alex Mac-Crue killed Zeke Hammer."

Jenny was appalled. "Killed him? But Alex hates guns. He doesn't even carry one. What are you saying? Did they force him into it?"

"It seems MacCrue killed the man in a fist fight."

Jenny was lying on her bed — something she never did unless she was ready to go to sleep — with a cold cloth on her forehead. She had cried for a long time, and had a pounding headache. She told herself, and it was true, that it was an accumulation of things — the shock of discovering what had actually happened to her sister and her husband, the strain of the reburial, and the constant talk of "the Sweetwater war" and — Alex MacCrue.

She heard a scraping sound at her window

and lay quiet, listening. It didn't come again. She got up and drew the curtains aside. There was no one there. She started to draw back when she noticed something on the sill. She opened the window and found a dirty bandanna soaked with blood. It was wrapped around a dead bird. She picked it up before she realized just what it was, and when realization came, she recoiled and threw the thing into the yard. Then she heard a low laugh.

"Who are you?" she demanded, although she already knew. She slammed the window and stood in the center of the room, thinking what to do.

To Jenny the Laredo Kid had always seemed like a boy with a disarming manner and an infectious grin who was always trying to put something over, so when he came scratching at her door at night with his importunities, as he had several times in the past couple of months, she was able to fend him off with exasperated good humor, as you would any other overly bold youngster with a talent for flim-flam.

But that laugh! It seemed to Jenny that it had insanity in it. She remembered the look in his eyes when he had accosted her on the hill. And the bloody token he had left on her sill. Jenny was suddenly filled with the conviction that the Laredo Kid had come to kill her, but why? Why?

She went at once to the back door of her

little house and threw the bolt, just as someone tried the knob and then jiggled it violently. There was a scratching at the door, and Laredo's strange voice: "Jen-neee."

"Go away Laredo, and stop bothering me. Now that's enough," she said. She went to the front door, but there was no key in the old-fashioned latch. She had never locked her door. The key, she thought. The key. Where is it? She tried the drawer of a little stand with curved legs and a marble top. The key wasn't there. Where had she seen it? In a kitchen drawer, the one with the odds and ends. As she turned toward the kitchen her eye caught a shadow passing by the side window, going toward the front porch. She rummaged quickly through the littered drawer. No key. Her fingers went through the miscellany again, more deliberately. Still no key. She went to the front door and leaned her weight against it.

"Laredo, go away. I'll call out," she said, trying to put as much exasperation and authority as possible in her voice.

The scratching came again, this time at the window. "Jen-nee." It was almost a whisper. She turned to glimpse a ghastly face at the window before it disappeared in the direction of the door.

"I have a gun," she shouted. Again she heard the strange, low laughter. It infuriated her, filled her with unreasoning rage. She jerked open the door and shouted, "Laredo, *leave . . . me . . . alone.*"

She hardly saw that he was standing there with his hands hanging at his sides, his head drooping, his face white, dead looking, like a grinning skull. She pushed at him fiercely and he went tumbling into the yard. Then she realized what she had seen. The Kid's clothes, from his shoulder all down his left side, were soaked, caked with blood. Jenny gasped and went toward him.

The Laredo Kid, who had come a long hard way with his shoulder wound seeping and clotting then bleeding again and seeping and clotting, sat up slowly and reached for his gun.

Alex MacCrue had been waiting for the Kid about a mile down the road from the town for three hours. He could hardly stay awake. He was exhausted and he hurt all over. He had wondered for the hundredth time what was keeping Laredo, when it occurred to him that the man might circle the town and come in the back way. He gave up his thought of meeting the Kid alone, in a private place. He spurred his horse and circled the town in a run.

He was a hundred yards away when he saw Laredo start to pick himself up from the ground, and fifty yards away when he saw the gun.

"Laredo," he bellowed, not realizing he was doing it. Laredo lurched to his feet and pointed the gun at Alex.

Alex realized he had made his second bad mistake in assuming that the Kid had only the rifle. He must have taken the gun from one of the dead men after he and Jimmy and Rocklin had ducked for cover. The Kid threw a shot just as Alex piled off of his horse, then he ran and stumbled into the street toward the saloon.

"Alex! No!" Jenny shouted.

Ten people saw it happen. The Laredo Kid stumbling backward down the street, firing wildly at Alex MacCrue. Saw Alex MacCrue walking deliberately and implacably toward the Kid, not even bothering to draw his gun. Saw Jenny running into the street shouting, "Alex, no! Please. Don't!" Ten fascinated people heard the click as the hammer of the Kid's gun hit an empty shell, saw Alex pick the Kid off the ground and start to shake him, saw the Kid go limp, saw Alex stare at him and drop him in the street.

The Kid lay very still. His heart, pounding weakly against little blood supply, faltered and stopped.

Jenny ran to Alex's side and he put an arm around her. They were both looking down at the Laredo Kid. "I'm sorry," Alex said. "I'm so sorry. I made a mistake. But, anyway, he's dead."

"Thank God," Jenny said.

Alex turned and looked at her for a moment. "Amen," he said.

"Thank God you didn't kill him," Jenny said.

The town of Sweetwater never did know just who it was that killed the Laredo Kid.

Chapter 13

Ed Belsher was in a rage of impatience and worry. It had been building for twenty-four hours, ever since the lookout had reported that three men had ridden out of MacCrue's place heading north toward the main road; and his men, mostly veterans of the ranch who resented the influx of gunmen who didn't do any work, were getting edgy. The appearance of the horse with Rooney's body didn't help.

"Where in the hell did it come from?" Belsher demanded when three of his men brought it to the front of the house.

One of the men, called Baldy because of his wild and profuse shock of hair, said, "Up there. It's that Rooney."

"I can see who it is," Belsher yelled. The men stared at him and glanced at each other. "Well, get him down. See if there's anything in his pockets. Notes, scribblings, anything."

There was nothing.

"How was he killed?" Belsher asked.

"Shot." Baldy said.

Belsher paced briefly. Rooney had been a careful and ruthless man. He wondered who could have killed him.

"You'll have to bury him," Belsher said. "Corky still hasn't seen anything?"

"Nope. I checked just a few minutes ago."

"What's keeping them?" Belsher was yelling again.

"How do I know," Baldy said. "It's a long ride down there and back."

"Dammit, they would have sent word if they ran into trouble."

Belsher stewed until two o'clock in the morning, then told Baldy, who was on the porch dozing, to turn the men out.

"Now?" Baldy asked.

"Yes, now. We're riding down there."

Baldy shrugged. "You're the boss."

It was early Saturday morning, still dark, when one of the riders for Hendryx who was coming in from the open range far below Sweetwater Valley saw Belsher's six gunmen ride out of the valley and around the tip of the eastern foothills. They were pretty far away, but he heard them coming. He dismounted, led his horse behind a large Yucca and stood still until the riders had passed. When he reached the ranch he roused the foreman and told him what he had seen.

"Into the desert? What's out there?" the ramrod asked grumpily.

"Nothing. That's why I—"

"All right, all right."

"Should we tell the old man?"

"He rode into town yesterday with Brennan. Said he'd be back about noon today." The cowhand waited for the foreman to make up his mind. "Go back out there and watch. Wait till you get word. If you see them come back in, you come in."

"Got it."

"Six you said. Did you recognize any of them?"

"No. Too dark. Too far away."

When Hendryx rode in and heard what his foreman had to say, he didn't hesitate. "All right," he said. "Tell the men we're riding. Send someone with word to Brennan and Rusty Mack and Purley White. I mean one man for each of them. Tell them to bring men and meet us at the southeast end of the valley as soon as they can."

"Suppose, uh . . . suppose one of them doesn't want to come?" the ramrod asked.

"Then maybe that'll tell us something. Git."

Thirty-five men in all rode out of the valley that afternoon, following the tracks of the six riders. There were other signs too, old signs mostly washed out by rain, but for the first time some of the men who had heard stories about a hidden valley began to wonder if they were true.

When they swerved toward the sharply rising hills where the buzzards were circling, they didn't believe what they found. Six bodies neatly laid out and covered with blankets held down by rocks and piled with desert brush. Only a small corner of the makeshift mausoleum had been torn away by the scavengers.

Some of the men ripped away at the brush and when the bodies lay exposed, the riders crowded in to look at them.

"Belsher's gunmen." Hendryx told Rusty Mack.

"They were at the saloon last night when MacCrue said he was going after the stolen cattle." Brennan said.

"You men back off some," Hendryx told the riders. "I want to see if we can find out what happened here. Give us a hand, Cherokee." Cherokee was one of Purley White's men, who, it was said, could read sign in the middle of a river.

Purley was not along. He had sent four of his men, though, and word that he was stove up because a bronc that was supposed to have been broken had tried to crush his leg against the corral fence.

Cherokee took his time, and Hendryx and Brennan went over the ground with him. It wasn't all that hard to see what had happened. "Six men on horses, standing there," Cherokee said. "Two men standing here."

Hendryx and Brennan nodded.

"That couldn't have been all," Hendryx said. He looked up at the rocks.

"Don't seem likely," Cherokee said. "But only two of the dead men were shot twice. The other four were shot just once."

"I don't believe it. They had help. Men in the rocks."

"Only one shot from the rocks, I think," Cherokee said. And in the rocks they found the two shells ejected from Jimmy's Remington repeater, the two places where the Laredo Kid had tumbled down the cliff, and the two lookout spots. No more.

Hendryx and Brennan were shaking their heads. "Two men, one of them Alex MacCrue, against six gunslingers?" Hendryx said to Cherokee. "Do you believe that? What were the six men doing? Just standing there?"

"It's what happened," Cherokee said. "Four men hit by .45 bullets. One of those was hit twice, and the fifth bullet came from up here. Three men killed with a .38, and one of them was hit again with a .45."

"Then if it was MacCrue, Jimmy could have been up in the rocks?"

"No doubt about it." Brennan said.

"Jimmy fired twice." He turned to Cherokee. "What did he hit the second time?"

"Might have missed." Cherokee said. "Then there was the man who fell down the cliff. He didn't move around much the first time. Maybe knocked out. Then he got up and leaned against a rock and fell the rest of the way. Maybe the other shot from the repeater winged him."

"MacCrue and Jimmy and one other man?" Hendryx asked.

"A man with new boots who didn't come down the desert trail with the two men." Cherokee said.

"MacCrue and Jimmy," Hendryx said. "Do you believe that, Brennan?"

"And the man with the new boots," Cherokee said.

"No," Brennan said flatly.

"It would make sense, if it was MacCrue all along." Hendryx said.

"No. It's got to be somebody else." Brennan said.

"But who, dammit? There isn't anybody else."

"What about the two lookouts? There were three men up there. Where are the two lookouts?"

"Maybe they're the men who rode off across the desert," Cherokee said.

While Hendryx, Brennan and Cherokee had been scouting the desert floor, Rusty Mack had taken his men and found the trail up into the valley, and one of the men had yelled down that there was something else they wouldn't believe.

While the cowhands were rounding up the cattle and prodding them a couple at a time down the rocky trail to the desert, Cherokee scouted the valley. Hendryx and Brennan nosed around the line shack and watched the cows coming in.

"Damndest thing I ever saw," Hendryx said.

"Took some planning," Brennan said. "Took a lot of help. Impossible for MacCrue."

"Near five hundred head," Hendryx said. "Yours, mine, Rusty's and Purley's and Belsher's. Not one of MacCrue's."

"Belsher would have figured that," Brennan said.

Hendryx nodded. "I wouldn't put anything past him."

Cherokee was gone over an hour, and when he returned he said, "Man with the new boots. I found where he came in. Over there. There's a hole through the rock, a tunnel. It goes through to the other side of the ridge."

"Who was he?" Hendryx asked.

Cherokee shook his head. "Don't know. Not

a cowboy. Didn't wear a holster. He crawled some in the grass; snake-crawled part of the way. No gunbelt. It was plain as day."

"A shoulder holster," Brennan said.

"For the thirty-eight," Hendryx agreed.

Rusty Mack rode up. "Couple more hours," he said, "and they'll have them all out. Three at the most. Found the dead men's horses, too. Someone must have brought 'em up."

"Rusty, could MacCrue be behind this?" Hendryx demanded.

"The rustling? The whole thing?" Rusty asked, incredulous.

"Yes."

"Not a chance in the world."

"This MacCrue." Cherokee said. "I don't think I've ever met him. Is he fast, good with a gun?"

"Hell," Rusty Mack said. "He doesn't even wear one." He turned to Hendryx and Brennan. "Have you ever seen him wearing a gun?"

"Come to think of it, I don't think I have," Brennan said.

"Never," Hendryx rumbled. Then he laughed. "Doesn't appear to need one. He killed Zeke Hammer with his bare hands in a saloon brawl last night."

"What?" Brennan said.

Rusty exploded. "You're loco, Hendryx."

"He did," Brennan said. "I was there with Hendryx. Saw the whole thing."

206

"What's your point?" Hendryx asked Cherokee.

"The men who killed the gunslingers, they were good. Very, very good. I can't believe how good they were."

"How can you be sure of that?" Hendryx asked.

"The gunslingers. Three of them didn't even fire their guns. Maybe four. I don't know about that because of the missing gun. But they were mounted, shooting downward, and I could only find two places where lead hit the ground."

Hendryx said, "The man who lost his gun when he fell off the ledge has the missing gun."

Brennan said, "The gunmen who got off the two shots, they must have been fast."

"No," Cherokee said. "That's what I mean. The two men facing the gunslingers would take them out as they drew, the fastest first."

"Hells bells, man, are you trying to say that the whole thing happened in the time it took two tardygrade gunslingers to pull iron?" Hendryx said.

"It looks that way." Cherokee calmly insisted.

Chapter 14

The sun was well up on a beautiful Sunday when Belsher and his men, riding south, encountered Hendryx, Brennan and Mack and their men pushing the cattle into the valley. The three ranchers rode to meet them, and they all moved aside, toward the hills, to let the point of the drive go by.

"Thought you might be down this way," Hendryx said to Belsher.

"Thought you would be too," Belsher said. "You heard MacCrue say he was going after the cattle. Where did he have them hidden?" He wondered about the Laredo Kid but didn't dare ask.

"You'd never guess," Hendryx growled. "And that might bring up the question of why you sent your gunmen down this way."

"They . . ." Belsher stopped. He had started to say that his men were following MacCrue, but something told him that would be a mistake. "Where else would I send them?" he said. "We've all been up and down this valley a dozen times. There's no place else to look." From a distance, he saw a man leading six horses carrying bodies. His men had seen them too. He looked back at the ranchers confronting him. "Didn't you run into them?" he asked.

"Not exactly," Hendryx told him. "We found them all shot to death."

Belsher turned pale. Then his neck swelled and he turned red. "MacCrue," he squeaked. "MacCrue and his gang."

"What gang?" Rusty Mack asked.

"He's got men. I know he has. Can't you see what happened? He led my men into a trap and killed them. Do you think that if I had my men guarding a stolen herd, they'd just let MacCrue's gang walk in on them? Where did you find them, anyway?"

"A high valley," Brennan said. "Completely hidden. Ever heard talk of a hidden valley?"

"Of course I have. And where's MacCrue? He said he knew where they were."

"He wasn't there," Hendryx said. "Nobody

was there. Just six dead men and their horses and the cattle."

"Then who else could have killed my men," Belsher yelled. "I'm going after him. Right now. He's the one who's responsible for all this and I can prove it. I'm going to have a showdown right now!"

"How can you prove it?" Hendryx growled.

"I can prove it," Belsher insisted. "Do I have to go alone?"

The three old ranchers hesitated. They had been around a long time, and had played a lot of poker. They could tell a man who had an ace up his sleeve.

"Give him some more rope," Brennan muttered.

"All right," Hendryx said, "Rusty?"

"Try to stop me," Mack said.

"Then we can tell the men to go home. The cattle can't wander off again." Brennan and Rusty nodded. Hendryx turned to the man leading the horses. "Tell the foremen they're through for the day. The men can go home, except I want Cal and Ringo." Cal was the best man with a six-shooter that rode for Hendryx, and Ringo was the gunman he had imported.

Rusty Mack sent for two of his men, and Brennan two of his. One of Brennan's men was dressed all in black, had no chaps, wore an ivory-handled forty-five and had obviously never done a lick of work in his life.

At about noon on that same beautiful Sunday, Jenny was leaving church; Alex MacCrue was leaving two horses at the livery stable to be fed and curried, and Rocklin was just rolling out of bed at the hotel after sleeping the clock around—and then some.

Rocklin was in no hurry. He shaved, washed himself standing up in a zinc washtub, laid out the clothes that the hotel had arranged to have washed and ironed, and neatly repacked his bedroll to accommodate his new cowboy boots. Then he went down to breakfast.

As he sat down he looked up the dirt street of the town and saw MacCrue taking Jenny's hand as she came down the two steps from her porch. It was an affecting sight, the young woman, still wearing her Sunday dress and all confidence, and the young man taking his courage in his hand even though he felt the eyes of the whole world on him.

In fact, many curious eyes had glanced at Alex MacCrue as he rode into town, left the livery stable to knock on Jenny Lee's door

212

and then continued down the street to meet her as she was starting home from church. She had been with a group of people, chatting, walking slowly away from the broad front yard of the church, where horses, a wagon, a couple of buckboards and even a shay were kicking up dust. As Alex had approached Jenny, his face noticeably red, she had glanced up, and the pink spots had appeared high on her cheeks.

"Morning," Alex had said, looking grim.

"Good morning," Jenny had said, smiling at him brightly.

The people with Jenny had said their polite good mornings and faded toward their destinations.

"They act as if I'm some kind of curiosity," Alex had grumbled.

"Why, they were just being considerate," Jenny had said. "They are my friends."

Several people had nodded or said good morning as they walked down the wooden sidewalk, and Jenny had replied in kind, calling each person by name. Alex had laughed shortly, not without humor. "Does everybody always go out of their way just to say good morning to you?" he had said.

"Of course they're curious," Jenny had said. "Some of them have never seen you before."

She laughed lightly. "Although certainly they have all heard of you. You have always been a subject of talk; now you're notorious." Alex had looked at her questioningly, and her expression showed slight surprise. "Why, aren't you the man who killed Ezekial Hammer with his bare hands?"

Alex was still brooding about that as he and Jenny were walking toward the stable.

"Try to put it out of your mind," Jenny said. "If you didn't even know . . ."

"I should have," Alex growled, thinking of Rocklin's lethal ways.

"But you didn't," Jenny insisted. "Now, this is a lovely day and we are going to have our first Sunday dinner. New England boiled dinner. It's the best I could do on short notice, but I'll make some corn starch pudding. Chocolate." She startled him by taking his arm as they crossed the street toward the stable. "Why are we going here? I'm not dressed for riding, Alex."

"I've got something to show you." He led out a sassy little bay mare, beautifully groomed, with a new bridle and side saddle. "She's for you."

Jenny was almost speechless. "But . . . but

. . . Oh, Alex she's absolutely beautiful. Oh! I love her." She threw her arms around the mare's neck. The horse, taking to her at once, nuzzled her.

"Her name is Princess," She told Alex. "Because right now I feel like one. Oh!" Alex couldn't have been more pleased, and he showed it, not caring that the stableman was watching.

"Oh, but I can't, Alex," she wailed, without any trace of guile.

"Why?" Alex was distressed.

"Well, I just . . . I mean, it's too much. I mean . . . Well, Alex, we're not even engaged!"

"What do you mean?" Alex was astonished. "Of course we are."

"But you haven't . . . I don't remember . . ."

Alex threw caution to the winds. He took her in his arms and said, "Jenny Lee, will you be my teacher and my love and my dear companion, always?" It was perfect. And Alex didn't even remember that he had read it in a book.

The stableman, an astute observer of the human scene who had been happily married for thirty years, marveled at how deftly, subtly, naturally, and even unknowingly, a woman takes hold of certain reins.

It was getting toward evening, and Rocklin was concerned. Alex was still sitting with Jenny on her front porch, and looked as though he planned to stay awhile. Finally, he walked to the stable, touching his hat to Jenny and Alex on the way, saddled Buck and rode out of town.

Alex was brooding again.

"You were going to stop thinking of Ezekial Hammer," Jenny said.

"I was thinking about somebody else. And thinking something must be wrong with me." Jenny waited. "There's a man," Alex said. "I owe him . . . well, everything. He saved Jimmy's life. He probably saved my ranch. He saved *my* life. And mostly what I feel toward him is resentment."

Jenny didn't say anything. She knew that this was a man's talk, a man's feeling, with all its irrationality. She wasn't worried. She felt that Alex would handle it, now that he had said it out loud. But the whole thing was completely outside her own experience.

"It's my fault, I suppose," Alex said. "It seems to me I've been alone all my life. I've thought about that a lot. It's going to

216

change."

"People, even people who have never met you, respect you a lot for what you have accomplished."

"But left me strictly alone."

"Isn't that the way you wanted it?"

"I reckon so." He gave his short laugh. "There were times, though, when I might have accepted an offer of help."

"I think you probably had more help than you know," Jenny said mildly. Alex looked at her with interest, and without resentment.

"What do you mean?"

"As I said, you were talked about. I've heard some of it. For years the ranch hands in the valley kept . . . oh, a casual eye, you might say, on your stock. Chased them back if they strayed too far; moved them with their own to new grass; brought some of them in at roundup; kind of kept them together. You know. The ranch owners told them to."

"Who told you that?" Alex asked.

"Why, no one in particular. It wasn't a secret."

"Why didn't anyone ever tell me?"

"Well because . . . I don't know. It's not something you *tell*, is it? I mean, these people . . . the people in this valley, they have a lot of good in them. They wouldn't *tell*, they would just do it."

Alex stood up abruptly and turned away. Jenny stayed very quiet.

Chapter 15

Rocklin and Jimmy were sitting on the steps talking when Alex rode in. Alex had been thinking about Rocklin, but he hadn't quite been prepared to see him sitting on the front porch.

"Did you know I had killed Zeke Hammer?" he barked at Rocklin. Jimmy's eyes popped wide open.

"Certainly," Rocklin said.

"You really did kill Zeke Hammer?" Jimmy asked in wonderment. "Some of the boys at school . . . did you *really?*"

"What's your trouble?" Rocklin asked. "If you're alive, Hammer's dead. And it holds true the other way around. It's that simple."

"How?" Jimmy asked.

"In the fistfight," Rocklin told him.

Alex glared at Rocklin. "It was just a lucky punch," he told Jimmy, "and that's all there is to it." The subject was closed. He turned to Rocklin. "How long have you been here? Did you ride in in broad daylight?"

"No one saw me," Rocklin said. "It was dark."

"Why," Alex asked. "Are you expecting something to happen?"

"Yes."

"What?"

"I don't know. Jimmy tells me he saw Belsher's men heading south at about three this morning. The showdown's coming. That's all I know."

"You expect them to ride in here?" Alex asked.

"Not exactly. But it wouldn't surprise me."

Alex had sent Jimmy to bed, reminding him of school tomorrow, and he and Rocklin were still sitting outside when they heard the riders coming.

"They're actually coming in," Alex said.

"And making no secret of it," Rocklin said. "That may be a good sign. There's probably someone else along besides Belsher. It's going to be up to you. I'll be inside the door, but I

220

don't want to be seen if I can avoid it. Can you handle it?" It was simply a question.

"I can try," Alex said, showing no resentment.

"If there's a lot of talk . . . what I mean is, if you get any chance, call him Mr. Beecher, as though it was a slip of the tongue."

"What?"

"Beecher. Just if you get the chance."

Jimmy, who hadn't been asleep, appeared on the porch, pulling on his pants and carrying a shotgun.

"Get some light, Jimmy," Alex told him. Jimmy brought two lanterns and two pine-pitch torches.

When the riders pulled up in a shallow arch around the porch, Alex was standing on the steps, Jimmy was on the porch holding his double-barrel shotgun, and Rocklin was standing just inside the door in the dark. There were sixteen men facing Alex.

"We want to talk," Belsher said.

"Then talk," Alex replied. Belsher and some of the other men started to dismount. "Don't get down," Alex snapped. The men stayed in their saddles. "This is no friendly visit, not at this time of night," Alex said. "What do you want?" Then he saw Rusty Mack. "Is that you Mr. Mack?" he asked.

221

"It's me," Mack said.

"Step down and rest awhile."

"Not just yet," Mack said.

"It's all over, MacCrue," Belsher blurted. "My men found the cattle and you killed them."

"What men?"

"It won't work, MacCrue. Six of my men found the cattle. The cattle are back. It's all over."

"I killed six men all by myself?" Alex asked.

"You had help," Belsher yelled.

It was an eerie scene. The flickering light on the faces of the men. Tired-looking faces with scruffy beards. Tired men whose work clothes were caked with a mixture of sweat and dust. Resolute men who had no intention of resting this night until they had put an end to the trouble in Sweetwater Valley.

"We know all about it," Belsher said, more calmly. "I told everyone about your water."

"My water?" Alex was nonplussed.

"Your artesian well," Belsher shouted. "All you had to do was wait for a couple of dry years, and you'd have the whole valley by the throat."

Alex laughed without humor. "Why you poor fool, if that was my plan, why would I

222

complicate it by stealing cattle? You ought to stop talking, Belsher; you're showing everybody your hand. Now I know why you wanted my place so much."

"You admit you've got the water?" Belsher was red and his eyes were protruding.

"Admit it? Admit what? The water is simply there. And as long as I have it, anyone else who needs it will have it."

"Son," Hendryx rumbled.

"Don't call me son," Alex snapped.

Hendryx actually laughed. "MacCrue," he said. "Belsher here claims to have proof that you robbed the stage."

"Oh?" Alex said. "What proof?"

Rocklin, standing inside the doorway, took a deep breath. It had been an incredible long shot, and it was coming in. The madman was actually walking into his own trap.

"The Laredo Kid saw you hide it. Right here on your ranch." Belsher said.

"That's a damn lie," Alex said, his voice flat. It was a direct challenge, one that couldn't be ignored. Two or three men edged their mounts away from Belsher, and Belsher actually put his hand on his gun. Hendryx and Brennan pressed in on either side of him.

"You're a coward," Belsher yelled, his voice raspy and shrill as he forced it through his blood-engorged throat. "You throw insults and you won't wear a gun."

"Show me proof or I'll put on a gun and say it again," Alex said.

"Can you find the money?" Hendryx asked Belsher.

"I can try. Laredo described the spot. I'll take some men . . ."

"And one of mine and one of Brennan's and one of Rusty's," Hendryx said. "Is that all right with you, MacCrue?"

"Give them a torch, Jimmy," MacCrue said. "Whoever finds it," he told the men, "just bring it back. Don't leave Belsher alone with it."

Belsher was almost choking with rage as the men rode off. Hendryx, Brennan and Rusty were looking curiously at Alex.

"What are you up to, son?" Hendryx asked. Alex shrugged and leaned against the porch post.

They all stayed just where they were until Belsher and the others returned. Except for one small incident. The gunman in black, who had been chafing under Alex's order to stay on his horse, got down and stretched.

"I said stay on your horse," Alex told him without heat.

"How are you going to make me?" the man

sneered.

"Shut up and get on your horse," Brennan roared. The startled gunman did as he was told. "You're on this man's ranch," Brennan told him.

A half-hour later the men rode back, and Belsher handed the leather dispatch case to Hendryx.

"Let Belsher open it," Alex said. He picked up one of the lanterns from the porch railing and handed it to Rusty Mack, who edged over to Belsher's side and held the light high.

There was no mistaking Belsher's expression when he opened the case. It was one of total astonishment. "What kind of trick is this?" he demanded. Then he looked at the documents and turned dead white. His eyes seemed to glaze over, and he shook his head as though he had been stunned by a blow.

"What the hell is it?" Hendryx demanded. Rusty took the papers from Belsher's hand and Brennan moved up to look.

"Claims," Alex said. "Phony homestead claims in the names of twenty people. And some deeds to what we all thought was open range, and a few other things. He's got everybody in this valley blocked off from water."

"It's a trick," Belsher said. *These* are phony. Where's the money? What did you do

225

with the money?"

"The money's safe. I've got it," Alex said.

"All right," Belsher said, his voice suddenly flat and calm. "It's a clever trick. I didn't give you credit for having any brains. But it doesn't change anything. The papers are obviously worthless, probably forged. How did you pull it off?"

Alex shook his head pityingly. "Tell me, Mr. Belsher, if you knew where the money was, why didn't you say so? The robbery was over a month ago, and the money belongs to the bank, which means the people of this valley."

"I didn't know. The Kid just told me lately."

"Lately? The Kid hasn't been seen for more than four days." There was silence. Everyone was listening to it. It had the quality of breath being held. Belsher thought it over. If the Kid wasn't at the hidden valley, then he had gone somewhere. He was out of the way temporarily.

"He rode in late last night from El Paso," Belsher said, his voice calm with confidence. "He got his gear together and left for Mexico."

Alex sighed. He felt no elation. In fact, he felt a little sick. "Laredo died of a gunshot wound early Saturday evening in Sweetwater. He fell dead in the street. A dozen people saw it," Alex said. "He won't be trying to kill any more boys."

Belsher felt the impact of many eyes. He was sweating, and his throat sounded hoarse and dry when he said, "That was a hunting accident."

"Was it? Like all the other killings?"

"What good would it do me—or anyone—to shoot a boy?"

"To get me to go looking for him so your men could ride into my ranch—which was just what they did. Isn't *that* right, Mr. *Beecher?*"

Belsher didn't speak. His hand went to the butt of his gun and stayed there. Men were staring at him, and there was a general restless movement among the riders crowded around. Jimmy's near death had been generally accepted as an accident. No one would deliberately shoot a boy.

Belsher turned slowly to his men. "Are you men with me on this? It's clear that they're going to railroad me. Well?" The men didn't move. Hendryx, to Belsher's right and slightly behind him, edged his horse closer. He had plucked a rope from his saddle and was quietly shaking out the loop.

227

"Seems like you've come to the end of your string, Mr. Beecher," Alex said. "I mean Mr. Belsher."

"So have you," Belsher said, and Alex, unarmed, could read the fierce, animal intent to kill in his eyes. Suddenly Belsher started to draw. At the same instant, Hendryx spurred his horse gently forward blocking the draw and almost in the same movement flipping the rope around Belsher's neck.

"The barn," Hendryx said. "We'll throw him out of the loft." There was movement in that direction, but Alex took the shotgun from Jimmy and fired a barrel into the air. Everyone stopped immediately and turned. Several men started to draw guns.

"No," Alex said. "Not on my place."

Belsher's men were backing off, starting to ride away, putting distance between themselves and the boss. The other men looked at Hendryx and Brennan and Mack. They were looking at Alex.

"I said not here," Alex repeated. "Get him off of my place." But he had not taken his eyes off of Belsher and he knew, he faced it, that it wasn't going to be that easy. The man hadn't moved; he hadn't appeared to have even noticed the rope. All signs of human feeling had left his face; it was like a death mask—except for the eyes.

The riders in the circle around Alex fell quiet. Those who had started to turn and ride away stopped and looked back, then eased their mounts around into the circle again and sat still. Hendryx nudged his horse away from Belsher.

Alex, staring at the face that had stopped being a face, was aware of the movement around him and what it meant. A corner of his mind wondered if this showdown had always been his, ever since the beginning. He had always been the target; and now this strange man staring back at him was going to kill him, without caring at all that it would be the last thing he ever did.

It was almost a shock to him when Belsher spoke. He hadn't expected it. Maybe there was a chance . . . No. No way out. For some reason the thought of Rocklin flickered across his mind.

"You killed him," Belsher said in a flat growl. "You killed my son."

Alex was aware of a stealthy movement to his right, where Blackie was sitting his horse. The sullen gunman—who had been put in his place—seemed to be moving even farther to Alex's right, almost flanking him. Would he mix in out of sheer meanness and spite? Alex

229

couldn't guess, but he shifted position slightly. Belsher didn't appear to notice.

In the house, in the dark just inside the door, Rocklin too spotted the movement, and shifted his position for a clear line of sight toward the lurking shadow.

"Laredo?" Alex asked.

"Laredo," Belsher replied.

Alex shook his head. "I didn't kill your son, Belsher, you did. You knew he wasn't all there and you turned him loose to kill. You probably taught him."

"Will someone give this man a gun." Belsher sounded as though he was about to choke.

Now, Alex thought.

Blackie drew one of his Colt's and cartwheeled it through the air toward Alex. Even before Alex had caught it with his right hand, Belsher started to pull his gun. Alex, who was half turned toward Blackie, tipped up the muzzle of the shotgun he held in his left hand and pulled the trigger, then he grabbed at the Colt and caught it by the barrel. As Alex flipped the Colt in his hand, Blackie drew — but he didn't get to fire. A shot from the doorway snapped his head back and at almost the same time Alex shot him full in the chest. Belsher's shot had hit the

230

edge of the porch where Alex stood, but it was his last one. His face had simply vanished, leaving a bloody skull, and he was slumping out of the saddle.

Later there was talk about the showdown at the Bar M, but for days it was strangely subdued, and those who had been there were not quite sure why. It could have been—partly at least—that the men who were there had to mull over, each in his own way, the fact that one man could be so crazy with ambition and greed as to cause all that killing. Or it could have been that many of them were not quite sure what actually happened. Yes, MacCrue had let go with his shotgun and caught Belsher full in the face; but could he have shot Blackie at almost the same time with a six-shooter he had practically picked out of the air? And especially since both Hendryx and Brennan had suddenly come alert and had blasted away at the gunman? Or was the silence part of a puzzled respect for Alex Mac-Crue, who did what he had to do while clearly hating it?

As for Alex, he never again spoke of the killings—except once, to Rocklin.

Chapter 16

Mary Tillman
17 Washington Square Place
New York City, New York

My Dear One,

I am sure this letter will precede me by only two or three days, but I wanted to assure you of my continued well-being and tell you that the special job I came here to do has been brought to a satisfactory conclusion.

I think one of the reasons I enjoy a trip West is that it is so pleasant to return to New York. I suppose it is true, too, that one reason I enjoy New York so much is that it is such a pleasure to leave and come back here.

I am leading up to something. I have commissioned a banker here to buy a piece of property for me if and when it is put up for sale. The banker's name is Higgins, and he has a son, a stock broker in New York, who lives just a few blocks from us in the Village. Isn't that remarkable? The property is a square mile with a roomy and well-built house on it. We can do almost anything we want to with the house; that is, if we get it.

I know we swore never to own another ranch, but this will be more like a winter home. If we acquire the property, I will take two or three years to fix it up just right. Meanwhile, there is an old fellow here, Whiskers by name, who I am sure will live at the place and look after it for us. He is a canny old man. You will enjoy him.

Young Bill would delight in this place, I am sure. It has horses, cattle, mountains and forests where there is game and "Wild West" adventure. And, of course, the whole valley would be in awe of little Louise. Such a sophisticated young lady! Still, when I think of the responsibilities that some young people carry out here, I wonder if that air of self-assurance that young people in the city affect is wholly warranted. In short, I think some time out here might have a salutary effect on our children.

Old man Wellington at Consolidated has

instructed me to buy the land where the potash is, but all of my powers of persuasion could not move him to buy Black Basin. I shall buy the basin myself, and one day, my dear, we shall be, not just wealthy, but very, very wealthy.

But, of course, what makes it all worthwhile is that I have you.

There are two things I want to do before leaving here, just errands, really, but I will do them on my way out. I will go to El Paso to buy the land, some of it from a railroad land office and some from a firm of real estate speculators, both of which, I am sure, have advertised their dreary property as the Garden of Eden. Then I will of course make sure of the mineral rights. I am afraid Buck will have a long trip on a train. I'll take along plenty of sugar.

I might as well stop off in Chicago to see Bannister at the Cattlemen's Association.

I will be counting the miles.

Give my love to the children.

I remain,

Your loving and *impatient* husband,

William R. Tillman

Chapter 17

"It's an awfully big undertaking," Jenny Lee said. "Are you sure you want to do it?"

"Yes I am," Alex said. "That is, if you . . . I thought you'd like it."

"I'd love it; it sounds wonderful. But it's so . . . Are you *sure*, Alex? What I mean is, you're not exactly used to having big parties, or anything like that . . ."

"I wish everybody in the valley could come to the wedding . . ."

"The church wouldn't hold them . . ."

"Then afterwards, they could all just come out to the ranch for your party."

"I could help. Earlier in the week. I could ask three or four of my friends to come out to the ranch with me and we could get everything ready. I know they'd love to." She looked at Alex mischievously. "And they could be my chaperones."

"I don't know, though," Alex began.

They were sitting side by side on Jenny's front stoop, where the whole town could see them, and they were, in fact, getting a lot of attention, open and discreet.

It was not the sort of attention that Alex MacCrue was comfortable with, but there was something behind his tolerance of it, inchoate thoughts and feelings that were changing his life irrevocably. Some of his inner twistings and turnings brought specific insights that were understandable enough, however. He realized he had been withdrawn and alone too long, and that, except for what he read, he knew very little of even the immediate world beyond his ranch. He had learned a little more — a lot more — in the past weeks, and although he had not assimilated it, he was excited by it — excited and hungry for more. It was the tide in the affairs of Alex MacCrue, and it was sweeping him along.

And there was dear, wonderful Jenny, who seemed so far beyond him in her knowledge of the world. She was open and friendly; she liked all kinds of people, and all kinds of people liked her. She understood things, things like . . . well, what to say and do. All he knew — and although it was of towering importance, he didn't think of it as anything special — was how to work with men. During a roundup he was all business, and taciturn in the extreme, but every cowpoke in the valley respected him and liked to work with him.

He wanted to offer Jenny everything he had, but he also wanted to enter her world, and so, incredibly, the idea of the party had been his.

"Tables, chairs. What would I fix to eat?" Alex said.

Jenny sighed. She just couldn't get enough air, she was so excited. She had a thought. "Did you know, Alex, there's someone who could really help; and I'm sure he'd be glad to."

"Who?"

"Mr. Brandt, of course . . . oh, but maybe you've never met him."

"I've seen him. I know who he is. He owns the hotel . . . I don't know . . ."

"We could ask him. He'd know just what to tell us."

"But it's his business. I mean . . ."

"Oh, I don't think he'd charge anything. He's really a very nice man. I worked for him, remember?"

"But I'd have to offer. It's his business."

"Then offer, of course. But I'm sure he won't take anything."

Mr. Brandt was indeed glad to help, not just because he was very fond of Jenny but because he saw an unusual opportunity for a grand display of his talents. He had suggestions about food, buying it and preparing it (he would be glad to help), refreshments, linen; about tables and chairs (Alex could bring a wagon into town and borrow some) and about a wedding cake (a beautiful one, made by him, that would be the talk of the valley). It would be the most memorable party ever.

Chapter 18

"And just who is Beecher," Alex asked.

Rocklin told him about the Colorado swindle.

"So that explains that," Alex said. "And Leek?"

"He'll be taken care of."

"Sure he will."

Alex, bone tired and at the same time exhilarated, was sitting on his front porch trying to pry the whole story out of Rocklin. The night before, both men had been moody and uncommunicative. Alex had merely invited Rocklin to bed down on the leather couch in the huge front room, and then he and Jimmy had turned in.

When Rocklin rolled out, Alex, with Jenny on his mind, had already ridden into town.

They had had no chance to talk. Now, Alex was pressing. Rocklin disliked post-mortems, but he felt totally relaxed for the first time in weeks and refused to be riled.

"All nice and neat," Alex said.

Rocklin didn't bother to reply.

"No doubt he'll turn up dead, and that will be that."

No reply.

"No complications. Everybody's satisfied."

No reply.

"Like Belsher, right? You pushed him to the limit, or had me do it."

"I doubt that you have ever seen the spectacle of a public hanging. Why are you growsing?"

"Some of them noticed, you know," Alex said. "Rusty Mack for sure, and the gunslingers. I saw them glance at the doorway two or three times before they left."

"It will give them something to talk about," Rocklin said. "You'll be famous. A man who disdains firearms and kills with his bare hands. A man suspected by the whole valley of killing six men at one time."

"That's not funny. And suppose they learn about you? That will *really* be something to talk about."

"Then we are in agreement?" Rocklin

242

asked. "I don't know anything about you, and you don't know anything about me."

Alex almost laughed. "You are probably the most ruthless man I will ever meet."

"And the nosiest," Rocklin said. "Did you and Miss Lee set the date this morning?" Alex hadn't told him he had gone into town to see Jenny.

"None of your business. The Sunday after school is out. You're invited."

Rocklin sighed. "I'm honored, Alex. Very. But it's time to go."

"Home?"

"Yes."

"You said you live in New York. What kind of place is it? Is there a good university there?"

"A very good one. Why?"

"Jimmy said once that he thought he would like to go to college."

"Do you agree?"

"Of course I agree. Why shouldn't I?"

"It happens that I teach a course at the university occasionally. I know some people there," Rocklin said.

"Is it possible, then?"

"I don't see why not. He'll probably have to take a year of preparatory work, though."

"Why?" Alex demanded.

Rocklin smiled and held up his hands as though to fend off an assault. "No reflection on Jimmy, or on Miss Lee. It's just that it's very competitive. Most of the lads in the freshman class will have had three or four years of prep school."

Jimmy, who had been crashing about in the kitchen, came out with coffee. "What about school?" he asked.

"Mr. Rocklin is acquainted with a university in New York. We were just talking about it. What's the name of it?" Alex asked.

"Columbia. One of the oldest and the best."

"Oh. I've read of it."

"What's New York like?" Jimmy asked.

Rocklin laughed. "Oh, that's a hard one to answer, Jimmy. You may think it is the most exciting place you ever saw, or the most disgusting. Maybe both at the same time. I'll tell you this, though, it's separated from the Sweetwater Valley by a hundred years in many ways. They just recently built the Pearl Street Power Station, and before long, the entire city will have electric lights. We already have a telephone in our house. Just a few months ago I took the family for a walk across the new Brooklyn Bridge. It's a miraculous concrete and steel structure higher than your canyon walls that stretches over a river from one city to another."

Rocklin was in an expansive mood. Also, he liked young people and enjoyed talking to them. He thought of his own children, with their quick minds and their inexhaustible curiosity, and he realized that he missed them, missed talking to them.

"Disgusting?" Jimmy asked.

"You see, Jim, it's like this," Rocklin said. "People are people everywhere. Sweetwater, New York City, Santa Fe, San Francisco, it doesn't matter. But if you took all the people in New Mexico, Arizona, and Colorado, and probably Utah too, and crammed them all into a space no bigger than this valley—imagine that!—then you would see all the human qualities all together at once.

"On the one hand there is all that concentrated energy and focus. I tell you, when you see it in a place like New York, and especially when you see the good results, it's like a world of magic. I mean it's like standing on the Brooklyn Bridge at night and seeing the reflections on the water, and the ships, and the buildings of New York and Brooklyn.

"On the other hand, there is misery and poverty and every kind of human rottenness you can imagine in the entire West. Except

245

there's no room for it, no place for it to hide. It's everywhere, like piles of garbage. There's no way you can escape from the effects of it.

"That's a modern city, Jim. You'll never see anything like it."

"If I came to New York could I live with you?" Jimmy asked.

Alex was astonished. "Get ahold of yourself, young 'un. Before you go to New York you'll have to brush up some on your manners."

"You can," Rocklin said, "and welcome. Although you might like to live in a dormitory for awhile with the other lads. It would be an entirely new experience for you."

When Rocklin was about to leave he said, "By the way, Alex, I'm going to buy Black Basin. There's oil there."

"Black Basin?" Alex asked. "You're daft, man."

"There's oil there. You'll never see a better investment. Do you want a few hundred acres of it?"

"A few hundred . . . Black Basin? No thanks, Rocklin. Thanks anyway, but no."

"Suit yourself," Rocklin said.

"Wait. Look. Do you need the money? If you do . . . what I'm trying to say is . . . well, I owe you . . . Look, anything I have is yours."

"No, no. Not at all. Plenty of money. I just thought . . . well, it's a good chance. Thought I'd tell you about it."

"You're downright serious." Alex said. "How much of it are you going to buy?"

"Oh, twenty square miles. The land company will be glad to get rid of it for fifty cents an acre."

"Twenty square miles? What do you see in it?"

"The future, Alex. An incredible future source of power."

"How far in the future?"

"Ten, fifteen, twenty years."

"And I can get two sections for six-hundred and forty dollars?"

"Not if you think it's crazy."

"But *you* don't think it's crazy?"

"No indeed."

"Listen Rocklin, if people find out about this I'll be laughed right out of the valley."

"No one will know. I'm going to form a land company. You'll simply have a share in it."

"Oh. Another thing," Alex said. "It seems the special agent from Santa Fe wasn't just a rumor after all. He rode into town last night. He was pointed out to me this morning."

247

"Is that right?"

Alex chuckled. "I'll be surprised if he learns a single thing."

"If you played your cards right," Rocklin said, "you might leave the impression around — without lying, I mean — that he's the mysterious third man who has been here all along."

Alex MacCrue laughed out loud, and Rocklin looked, and felt, very pleased.

Alex was slowly shaking his head in mock disbelief. "You know, Rocklin," he said, "you are the most . . ." But he gave it up as hopeless.

It was early the next morning, when Rocklin was riding south out of the valley, that he turned east and rode into Purley White's place. Nobody challenged him, but someone had clearly alerted Purley, who was waiting at his door.

"Mornin' Mr. Rocklin."

"Morning."

"Step down," Purley said. "Find what you've been looking for?"

"Yep."

"Come in and tell me about it."

"I'll show you." Rocklin took the heavy

manila folder out of his saddlebags and followed Purley into the house. Purley was quiet as he poured coffee. When he had sat, he looked at the folder and then at Rocklin, his face expressionless. Rocklin took the documents out and handed them to the gnarled old rancher. Purley glanced at them, looked at Rocklin, and then went through them carefully, page by page. Rocklin imagined that he looked older when he had finished.

"Why are you showing these to me?" he asked.

"Aren't you the one who sent the emergency message to Chicago?"

"So they know." Purley said.

"The association doesn't know." Rocklin said. "No one knows."

"I didn't know what to do, Rocklin. By the time the killing started, Belsher had me by the short hairs.

"All right, I admit it looked good when Belsher first laid it out. I agreed with him, in a way. There just isn't going to be six ranches left in this valley in another ten years. It's as plain as day. Two or three spreads are going to have it all. Why, every man in the valley, except MacCrue maybe, has been buying quarter sections from homesteaders who couldn't make it, or were just in it for the profit. Then there were the preemption claims that gave the squatters more quarter sections. They cost a dollar twenty-five an acre, and I know a couple of the ranchers who were supplying the money! Don't you see?"

"I see."

"I knew somebody was going to get squeezed and I didn't want it to be me. All right, I got greedy. I was wrong. I was a damn fool. What a fool! The minute the killing started, I knew Belsher was going to go after all of it. The only reason he needed me in with him at all was that my place is so close to this end of the hills that I couldn't fail to see that cows were wandering out into the desert! And where to?"

"If no one ever finds out about your part in the whole thing, what are you going to do about these?" Rocklin asked, indicating the documents.

"I'll set everything as right as I can. Even if I lose my own place."

"Why should you?"

"I'm strapped. If I can't pay off some debts after spring roundup, I might be foreclosed." He shook his head as though chasing away gnats. "But that doesn't matter. I'll drop my options on the land to the south, and just leave my land in the valley as open range.

250

"But, hell, Rocklin, I don't know what good it will do. Half the damn valley is in private hands right now!"

"And Belsher was going to fence it off," Rocklin said.

"What?"

"But Belsher's dead. The house of cards is coming down. Probably the only thing left with a clear title will be the ranch."

"Belsher had a wife in Denver," Purley said.

"He did? Same name?"

"Yes."

"Will you do something for me, Mr. White?"

"Just tell me what it is."

"If you go into town in the next week or so . . ."

"Going in tomorrow."

"Good. Give Higgins a message and tell him it's from Rocklin. Tell him Belsher had a wife, a lawful wife of the same name, in Denver. Did he have any children?"

Purley shook his head. "None except the Laredo Kid."

"You knew about him?"

"Sure did."

Rocklin sighed. "Well, that's it. Good luck, Mister White."

"Why are you doing it this way, Rocklin? I

don't deserve any consideration. So why?"

"You had no part in all the killings?" Rocklin asked. "And by the way, what about the killings?"

"If anyone got too close or stumbled onto something, he was killed, that's all. I had nothing to do with that. But the fact is, I didn't have the sand to speak up."

"Well, you see," Rocklin said, "in a way, I was working for you. You got me here. And also, if your part in it never comes out, my part in it will never come out."

"I see," Purley said. "I'll be damned."

Rocklin smiled slightly. "A man can't be too careful."

It took Rocklin three days to wind up his business in El Paso. And, it seemed, almost that long to coax Buck onto the train. When the train was rolling, Rocklin sat back and closed his eyes. He was exhausted, but he was satisfied.

When the people of Sweetwater Valley learned that Rocklin had bought Black Basin they thought it was very funny. They called it Rocklin's folly.

BEST OF THE WEST
from Zebra Books

THOMPSON'S MOUNTAIN (2042, $3.95)
by G. Clifton Wisler

Jeff Thompson was a boy of fifteen when his pa refused to sell out his mountain to the Union Pacific and got gunned down in return, along with the boy's mother. Jeff fled to Colorado, but he knew he'd even the score with the railroad man who had his parents killed . . . and either death or glory was at the end of the vengeance trail he'd blaze!

BROTHER WOLF (1728, $2.95)
by Dan Parkinson

Only two men could help Lattimer run down the sheriff's killers—a stranger named Stillwell and an Apache who was as deadly with a Colt as he was with a knife. One of them would see justice done—from the muzzle of a six-gun.

BLOOD ARROW (1549, $2.50)
by Dan Parkinson

Randall Kerry returned to his camp to find his companion slaughtered and scalped. With a war cry as wild as the savages,' the young scout raced forward with his pistol held high to meet them in battle.

THUNDERLAND (1991, $3.50)
by Dan Parkinson

Men were suddenly dying all around Jonathan, and he needed to know why—before he became the next bloody victim of the ancient sword that would shape the future of the Texas frontier.

Available wherever paperbacks are sold, or order direct from the Publisher. Send cover price plus 50¢ per copy for mailing and handling to Zebra Books, Dept. 2385, 475 Park Avenue South, New York, N.Y. 10016. Residents of New York, New Jersey and Pennsylvania must include sales tax. DO NOT SEND CASH.

BOLD HEROES OF THE UNTAMED NORTHWEST!
THE SCARLET RIDERS
by Ian Anderson

#1: CORPORAL CAVANNAGH   (1161, $2.50)
Joining the Mounties was Cavannagh's last chance at a
new life. Now he would stop either an Indian war, or a bullet — and out of his daring and courage a legend would be
born!

#3: BEYOND THE STONE HEAPS   (1884, $2.50)
Fresh from the slaughter at the Little Big Horn, the Sioux
cross the border into Canada. Only Cavannagh can prevent
the raging Indian war that threatens to destroy the Scarlet
Riders!

#4: SERGEANT O'REILLY   (1977, $2.50)
When an Indian village is reduced to ashes, Sergeant
O'Reilly of the Mounties risks his life and career to help an
avenging Stoney chief and bring a silver-hungry murderer
to justice!

#5: FORT TERROR   (2125, $2.50)
Captured by the robed and bearded killer monks of Fort
Terror, Parsons knew it was up to him, and him alone, to
stop a terrifying reign of anarchy and chaos by the dead-
liest assassins in the territory — and continue the growing
legend of The Scarlet Riders!